Dear Reader,

First of all, let me c[...]
heroine, Kenna Ma[...]
problem. As I have [...]
ask anyone, especially my husband and editor;
they'll be happy to confirm this as fact—you'd
think she would have been easy to write. Nope.

Kenna Mallory just didn't want to conform. She
had to torture me the entire way. She didn't want
to wear what I wanted her to wear, didn't want to
say what I wanted her to say and she didn't want
to fall in love because I said she should.

I'm afraid she didn't torture just me. She
tortured everyone she came in contact with—
her family, her co-workers and especially one
Mr. Weston Roth, the man sharing her position
on the corporate ladder.

But don't feel too sorry for Wes. Tall, muscled
and sharp as a tack, he thought he had Kenna all
figured out. Unfortunately he was wrong. As a
matter of fact, he was a lot wrong. Ah, the mess
these two had to go through before they came
to somewhat of a shocking realization.

What realization, you ask? You'll have to read to
find out. I'll give you one hint—this is a romance!

Happy reading!

Jill Shalvis

P.S. I love to hear from readers! Come visit my
Web site at www.jillshalvis.com to drop me a line
and to check out my new releases.

"What did he do, threaten to cut off your credit card?"

If Wes had been any closer, Kenna's look would have fried him on the spot. Good thing he stood a healthy distance from her.

"I don't care about my father's money," she enunciated slowly.

"Really." Wes found that hard to believe, given the evidence to the contrary. "So, if not the money, what *do* you care about?"

"Not his money," she repeated. "I earn my own. As for what I do care about... I care about my life. Living it how I want to, which until now has been very different than this structured, cutthroat business atmosphere. How about you, Mr. Roth?"

"Wes."

"Okay. *Wes,*" she said with an acknowledging bow of her head. "What is it you care about?"

"This structured, cutthroat business, for one."

She actually laughed, completely defusing the charged atmosphere between them. "Well, that's going to make us quite the interesting pair."

Blond
Natural ∧ Instincts
JILL SHALVIS

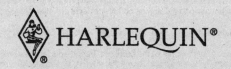

HARLEQUIN®

TORONTO • NEW YORK • LONDON
AMSTERDAM • PARIS • SYDNEY • HAMBURG
STOCKHOLM • ATHENS • TOKYO • MILAN • MADRID
PRAGUE • WARSAW • BUDAPEST • AUCKLAND

ISBN 0-373-44179-7

NATURAL BLOND INSTINCTS

ABOUT THE AUTHOR

Jill Shalvis has been making up stories since she could hold a pencil. Now, thankfully, she gets to do it for a living, and doesn't plan to ever stop. She is the bestselling, award-winning author of over two dozen novels, including series romance for both Harlequin and Silhouette. She's hit the Waldenbooks bestsellers lists, is a 2000 RITA® Award nominee and is a two-time National Reader's Choice Award winner. She has been nominated for a *Romantic Times* Career Achievement Award in Romantic Comedy, Best Duets and Best Temptation. Jill lives in California with her family.

Books by Jill Shalvis

Dear Reader,

A brand-new year is around the corner and once the holiday celebrations are over, it's time to make resolutions. And this time, ignore those pesky ones you never really pay attention to! Instead, make sure to give yourself a break from your troubles. Relax and unwind—with a Harlequin Flipside novel! These clever and witty stories blend comedy and romance in a way that's sure to smooth away any tension....

In December, award-winning author Jill Shalvis brings us *Natural Blond Instincts*, a story about an independent woman who finally has the chance to prove to her conservative family that she can succeed in the family business. Of course, the gorgeous man who shares her position is so distracting she's having trouble focusing on the job!

We also have *Who Needs Decaf?* by Tanya Michaels. Given the stress of her life, this PR exec needs large injections of high-octane java to get through her day. Too bad the caffeine isn't having an effect on her love life. At least, not before she meets the good-looking guy who's determined to dig up dirt on her company....

Look for two new Harlequin Flipside novels every month at your favorite bookstore. And be sure to check us out online at www.harlequinflipside.com.

Have a Happy New Year and enjoy!

Wanda Ottewell
Editor

Mary-Theresa Hussey
Executive Editor

1

KENNA MALLORY thought she'd turned out okay, though she supposed that depended on who you asked. Zipping alongside the Pacific coast just outside Santa Barbara, the sun at her back, the radio blaring...she herself couldn't have asked for more.

But her parents...undoubtedly they could have filled volumes on how they might have changed their only daughter. Changed and molded and created.

Unfortunately, they'd blessed Kenna with her own mind. Hence, the Mallory family issues. She didn't toe the line, she didn't follow the rules, she didn't fit the mold. *Their* mold.

Which explained the slightly exasperated voice of her father in her ear, courtesy of the cell phone she'd won in a mail sweepstakes.

"Kenna, honestly. You baffle me." This was said in a paternal tone suggesting impatience, superiority and that mind-boggling emotion called love. A powerful combination on the best of days, designed to crank the guilt factor up to maximum overload. "I've got the perfect job for you, and you have no response."

None that he wanted to hear, anyway.

Since he'd been doing his damnedest to run her life from the moment she'd been born, and she'd been doing her damnedest not to let him, the result had made for some interesting arguments over the past twenty-seven years. "Dad...thank you. I appreciate it, but I've got my own job, remember?"

"Washing crap out of poodles' tails is not a job, Kenna."

She glanced at the waves pounding the shore because it was calming, and at the moment, she needed calming. "I don't do that anymore and you know it." She purposely avoided reminding him exactly what she did do for a living. Did she really need to say—again—that she wasn't in his world because he'd kicked her out of it?

Since then, sure, she'd had some, uh, *creative* jobs to earn her way through college. But recently, she'd landed herself a position in the accounting department of Nordstrom's. One thing she'd gotten from Kenneth Mallory, III, was her love of business and finance. She was good at it. So good, in fact, that on her better days she'd call herself a whiz.

"The job I have for you is important," he said.

"As opposed to, say, slinging beer at that bar where the women wear those tight white tank tops."

"Now, you *know* I only did that for one week." And she'd made enough money to cover an entire semester's tuition. Who could complain about that?

"Kenna, for once, *listen.*"

"Fine." She pretended his tone didn't sneak past her defenses and stab at her. Was it so bad to want to make her own way? To want to be successful and please him at the same time, without compromising herself and her beliefs just because they were different than his?

"You're a Mallory—"

Oh yeah, here it came. The Mallory card. She could recite it verbatim. *As a Mallory, you owe it to the family... As a Mallory, you must present yourself this way... As a Mallory...*

Never mind that she didn't consider herself a Mallory, and that she hadn't for a long time. It wasn't the name she minded, but the baggage attached to it that she could definitely live without. She just wanted to be her own person.

Her own person who lived quite happily in a four-hundred-square-foot studio apartment in Santa Barbara. Sure, she had neither an adequate bathroom mirror nor a tub, not to mention only enough closet space for one pair of shoes, but she had her pride and her freedom, and she valued both. "I just really want to manage on my own."

"*Want* has little to do with family obligation. Remember your great-great-grandfather Philippe, who—"

"—came over on the boat from France with only the clothes on his back," she intoned along with him. "Walking to work every day in the icy, freezing snow, ten miles uphill each way—" She stopped when she heard his reluctant chuckle.

"Okay, so I've mentioned him before."

"Only a few billion times." She smiled at his admission. "I get it, Dad, honest. We work hard. But I *am* working hard, just not for you."

"It doesn't make sense. Explain it to me. Make me understand."

As she came into Santa Barbara, a sprawling, hopping, happy beach town that liked to party, the glittering summer sun set its edges down on the ocean, creating a glorious end to the day. Never one to pass up a sky-gazing moment, Kenna shoved her sunglasses to the top of her head to see better. "Well, for starters, you and Mom live in San Diego."

"Not a good enough excuse."

"It's four hours away, Dad."

"Like you've never moved before."

"Well then, how about because we spontaneously

combust if we're together in the same room for more than five minutes?"

"So we've had a few obstacles in our day. That's no reason to stop trying."

Obstacles. Meaning, of course, her wild and crazy years. The years Kenna had spent battling her insecurities and inadequacies in the face of her brilliant parents had been long and rather ugly. But she'd paid the price—dearly—when, at the age of eighteen, she'd had all funds yanked from beneath her feet, leaving her as accused.

Wild and crazy.

And penniless.

It had been their version of tough love, and it had been tough. Extremely so. But she hadn't been born a Mallory for nothing. Stubbornness and tenacity had been bred into her, and she'd marched off to college determined to prove she could manage on her own. She'd been the principled, idealistic rebel, an activist on campus staging sit-ins at the administrative building whenever she thought an injustice had been committed.

She'd horrified her parents on a weekly basis, but because they'd already overplayed their hand by cutting off the money, they were powerless to do anything about her actions. With such freedom in front of her, she'd never looked back, not until the day she'd graduated.

Granted, she'd graduated by the skin of her teeth, at a far less prestigious school than her parents had planned on, but she *had* finished. She'd done it on her own, grooming poodles, doing the aforementioned "slinging beer," mopping up at K-Mart, you name it, she'd done it for the little luxuries like food and tuition. She'd done it because she'd wanted to, and because she figured her parents had not expected her to. They probably had planned for her to last a week—two, tops—without their financial support. Then, when she came begging for money, they could have pulled out the Mallory family rule book, forced her to agree to follow said rules in exchange for that support and signed the whole deal...in blood. One more time their rebel daughter had not performed according to plan.

Her father had tried to get her to work for Mallory Enterprises after graduation. *Pick one of our hotels,* he'd told her. *Take an entry-level position and learn the ropes.*

It had been a decent idea. After all, she'd studied the hotel industry in college, but the bottom line was that their ideologies clashed. Her parents were conservative fiscally and socially, whereas she was about as liberal as you could get.

They thought in terms of dollars.

She thought in terms of people. She believed minimum wage should be high enough that everyone could live without hunger and poverty. They'd like to see minimum wage abolished.

Clash, clash, clash.

"You're ready for this now," her father said. "Taking over this newest acquisition for us is just the beginning for you at Mallory Enterprises. Admit it, you love business the way your mother loves performing surgery. You'll be a natural."

"I don't have the image."

"You're a Mallory, aren't you?"

"Maybe I meant *physical* image." She certainly *could* have meant that. At fifty-eight, her father defined *elegant* and *sophisticated*, a self-made man who had turned a small fortune into millions. Her mother could have passed for a young Audrey Hepburn...who just happened to be a brilliant surgeon.

And then there was Kenna. An untamed blonde. A good six inches taller than her parents and stacked to boot. Her Saxon looks were a throwback to the grandmother she'd never gotten to meet.

"I understand there will be a learning curve," her father said, most likely referring to the reforming of her strong-willed, strong-minded and, on the best of days, somewhat unpredictable nature. "Think of it,

Kenna. Working for me, you could buy that Ferrari you always dreamed of. Maybe I'd even buy it for you."

Oh, now that wasn't fair, using an old fantasy against her. She hadn't dreamed of having a Ferrari since she'd been sixteen years old. She tapped the steering wheel of her extremely old Honda Civic and tried to remember how many third-world countries could be fed on the price of one fancy-schmancy car.

"How's this," her father proposed. "A vice president position. You can run things, as you want."

Treacherously, her heart leaped. Vice president...

"I'll expect you in one week at our latest acquisition, the San Diego Mallory. We picked it up eighteen months ago. It just reopened after major renovations. You'll be working with a Mr. Weston Roth. The two of you will run the place together."

Vice president definitely had a better ring to it than her current position—accounting clerk, level one.

"You and Roth are a partnership made in heaven, trust me."

"I thought this was *your* baby," she said.

"No, no. It's Weston's. He's been acting VP since Milton Stanton retired last year. And now, with your education under your belt and your silly roaming the planet habit out of your system, it's yours as well."

She'd "roamed the planet" for six glorious weeks as a travel scout for a travel agency just outside of Los Angeles, and she'd worked her tush off. But while business, and more specifically, numbers, were her thing, organization and travel writing were not. She'd failed horribly. "I don't think so, Dad. I'm sorry."

"No, I understand." Her father's voice lowered. Sounded sad. "It's just that you're an only child. The business is massive. Hotels scattered throughout the West. If something were to happen to me or your mother..."

She flicked off her radio, her chest suddenly tight. "Okay, what's the matter?"

"It's...nothing."

"Is one of you sick?"

"If I pretended to be, would that count?"

She let out a relieved breath. "I know you didn't have me just so that I'd take over your business."

"You're really going to let this multi-million dollar corporation go to your cousin Serena simply because it's not your thing?"

Serena was deeply entrenched at Mallory Enterprises, working in conference sales and management, and very happy there. She could have the place *and* Kenna's new partner, Mr. Weston Roth, as far as Kenna was concerned. Just his name evoked images of an old, stern, hard and unforgiving man.

She hated stern, hard, unforgiving men.

"Please, Kenna. Please do this."

Wow, he'd hauled out the magic word, which to her recollection, he'd never used before.

"Try it," he cajoled. "Give me...say, six months."

Just give up her life in Santa Barbara for six months to work in San Diego, two hundred and fifty miles away. Like *that* was easy to do. It wasn't San Diego that was the problem—she loved the exciting beach town nearly as much as she loved Santa Barbara. It was the thought of once again being under his thumb, following his rules...

And yet, something was new here. He was *asking* her, not telling.

As she'd secretly wanted all her life to please him, please him while still being herself, it made her hesitate. "What happens at the end of the six months?"

"If you're not cut out for the job, I'll be man enough to admit it."

"You mean that?"

"I just said so, didn't I?"

Yes, shockingly enough, he had, and Kenna had never known him to go back on his word. "I'll drive you crazy," she said, and held her breath.

Deny it, she silently wished. *Deny it*.

"Only if you're inadequate."

She let out the breath and resisted banging her hand on the steering wheel. Her gut churned because she'd always yearned to show him exactly how her creative and inventive ways could be channeled into something good, something worthwhile, something that would please them and herself at the same time.

She was insane, but... "Okay."

"Okay?"

"Okay, I'll do it." What the hell, six months wasn't a life sentence. And it would be nice to be able to afford good hair products again. "If I can do it my way."

He hesitated for a long moment. "We're talking aboveboard, right? All legal-like?"

She rubbed her temples. "Yes, Dad. All legal-like."

"Well, then. Perfect."

"And after six months, I'm free to go."

"Unless you like the job."

Insanity, that's what this was, but Kenna couldn't pass up the chance to show him she could be strong, she could know her own mind and still fit into their world if she chose to.

She just couldn't believe that she was choosing to.

2

KENNA SPENT the week shifting her life from Santa Barbara to San Diego. It was surprisingly easy, because as it turned out, there were lots of people waiting in line to get her Nordstrom's job and fabulous employee discount.

She'd been far more expendable than she thought. A bit of a blow to her ego, but that made her more fiercely determined to succeed somewhere else. And that somewhere else might as well be within Mallory Enterprises. For now.

By the following Monday morning, she was a little more nervous than she would have liked as she made her way down the ornately decorated hallway of the latest Mallory acquisition, the San Diego Mallory. She supposed that could be directly related to the fact she had never really fit in with her family, so she had no idea what made her feel she could fit in here.

Well, screw 'em. She didn't need to fit in. She just needed to do her job and do it right. As a mood bolster, she wore her favorite pair of strappy high-heeled shoes with her suit, both in her favorite shade of fuchsia. Not exactly a Mallory corporate color, but she wasn't a black-suited, sedate sort of girl, so no use pretending.

She moved down the freshly polished floor, taking in the extraordinary antiques from all over the world that lined the walls of Mallory hotels, her watch mocking her—8:07 a.m....

She hated to be late, hated it. Her heels clicked as she picked up her pace, her purse banging her hip as she went. The building's striking architecture and stature were synonymous with the Old World charm and elegance that would appeal to the discerning business and social elite who made up the clientele of Mallory Enterprises. This hotel would fit right in.

Good for it.

Not wanting to skid into her first meeting, she slowed down and took a deep cleansing breath that didn't help as much as it should have. She tugged at the skirt that kept creeping upward, given the lack of a slip.

The lack was her mother's fault. Kenna had come down from Santa Barbara the night before and had stayed in her old bedroom at her parents' house. She hadn't lived there since the day she'd graduated from high school, and there'd been a good reason for that—aside from getting cut off financially, that is. Her parents had complete and utter disregard for her privacy. Just this morning while Kenna had been in the shower, her mother had set out a black suit on the bed, complete with nylons. *Nylons.* Now there was an item of clothing that had not been invented by a woman.

She'd given her mother back the suit and nylons, and the look on her face had made Kenna want to wear underwear with holes in it.

Or a fuchsia suit.

But by then, she'd been running late, and hadn't spared the time to locate her slip in the mess of her as-yet-unpacked suitcase.

So here she was, at the designated conference room on the second floor of the San Diego Mallory. All she had to do was go in and rattle off her readiness to discuss acquisition and renovation budgets, quarterly forecasts and long-term strategic planning—she'd been boning up, reading such fun and light fare as the corporation's annual reports and tourism stats for a week now—and she'd be set.

She had no doubts. She *could* do this. Hell, she'd once cleaned iguana cages at the LA Zoo, with the little buggers still in residence, so really, she could do anything. As she established herself here, she'd lighten up the uptight work atmosphere if she could. And she'd keep her sense of humor firmly in place, no matter what.

In light of that, she'd wow this old Mr. Roth, wow and dazzle...whatever it took. She put her hand on the door handle and noted that her heart had picked up speed and she was feeling a little overheated. Damn the nerves she didn't want to admit she had. Given that she'd promised herself never to let 'em see her sweat, she peeled off her jacket. Ready now, she opened the door and called out, "Honey, I'm home." She took a step inside and...went utterly still.

Twelve men wearing conservative dark suits sitting around a huge conference table stopped talking and turned her way. One of them was her father.

Fabulous. So much for her private meeting with Weston Roth.

Silence reigned for far too long as twelve pairs of eyes stared at her. She was just contemplating how to make a safe retreat when one of the suits stood up.

"I'll take it from here," he said, which she resented the hell out of.

No one would take "it" from here, not if they were referring to her.

That man came forward, and gestured to the door. "Shall we?"

"Sure." She smiled, having no idea who he was, but she could fake banalities as well as anyone. Attitude could come later in private.

He shut the door behind them while Kenna feigned a huge interest in the art on the walls, idly wondering who purchased their art. Did they go to the auctions? Private sales? In either case, no doubt they got ripped off.

The man who'd brought her out here simply watched her, she could feel his eyes boring into her back, so she turned around in order to eye him right back. His broad shoulders propping up the far wall, his long legs casually crossed, he looked for all the world as if he'd just strutted off the glossy pages of GQ magazine. Style, elegance and yes, dammit, the dreaded polish poured off him with ease. Clearly comfortable in his own skin, he smiled, and it wasn't a particularly nice one.

Kenna's resentment against him rose. She should have known this wasn't going to go well when she'd seen all the dark colors in the room. She had this theory that the colors people wore indicated their openness to new ideas, their ability to change. And what had she seen in the conference room? Unimaginative colors. Blah colors. She'd been the only splash of life in the room.

"So..." He cocked his head. "Where should we begin?"

"I'm not sure *we* have anything *to* begin." How had it come about that she'd agreed to this insanity?

Oh yeah, she'd decided she could do anything and might as well prove it to the world. Dammit, this whole mess was her own fault.

How she hated to admit that.

But one thing about growing up so quickly, about learning how to survive on her own, she'd also matured. Learned how to handle herself in just about any situation, including this one.

With a flick of his wrist, he glanced at his gold watch. "You know, you're not actually not that far off, time-wise. I have to admit to being a bit surprised on that score." Mr. Cool wore perfectly perfect creased dark-gray trousers and a perfectly perfect matching silk shirt that complemented his tall, leanly muscled form. Even his shoes screamed *sophistication* and had probably cost more than her entire wardrobe, most of which she'd picked up thanks to her Nordstrom's discount or her favorite hobby—consignment shops. She couldn't help it, she loved old things, particularly the glamour and style of the mid-twentieth century. Not that this man would know anything about that. He wore a pair of the latest wire-rimmed glasses, so completely in vogue she wondered if they were even prescription. Behind his lenses blazed a set of dark-blue, intelligent eyes that warned her not to underestimate him.

Actually, Kenna usually enjoyed intelligent men. She loved to talk, loved to debate, but in her world—correction, her *father's* world—intelligence couldn't compensate for lack of a sense of humor or a basic interest in anything outside of business, both of which were incredibly important to her.

This man, whoever he was, epitomized Mallory Enterprises just by standing there in his dark colors. He made her feel conspicuous and out of place. The only thing slightly redeeming him was that he seemed willing to talk to her at all.

Until he said, "I'm okay with you running out of here, if you'd like. I'm not really up for dealing with the boss's spoiled daughter anyway."

While that made her see red, a welcome color in this place, she managed to stay calm. "Who the hell are you?"

"Sorry." He pushed away from the wall, seeming even bigger now, and held out his hand. "Weston Roth."

Okay, so he wasn't ancient, wasn't a fuddy-duddy and she was quite certain she hadn't wowed or dazzled. Looked like their working relationship was off to an interesting start. "Well, Weston Roth. What do you say we make our first compromise. I'll forgive and forget the spoiled-daughter statement, and the fact that you're a pompous ass for saying it, if you'll forgive me for being all of seven minutes late." She slipped her hand in his, a little surprised by how big and warm it was.

He started to say something, but from behind the conference room door came the distinct sounds of men rising from their seats.

Followed by muted voices and...*footsteps.*

The dark suits were coming this way. Terrific. She didn't want to deal with her father right now. "What do you say we take this little meet-and-greet into one of our offices?" she asked a bit hastily.

"Sure." He gestured with his head which way to go, and kept up with her stride for stride. His smug smile told her he knew who she was avoiding and why, and it made her want to trip him.

She could handle this, she reminded herself as they walked. She could handle this and him.

She could handle anything. And if she said it often enough, it just might be true.

SHE WALKED into his office ahead of him, eyes flashing and chin high in the air, as if she wasn't wearing a skirt better suited for swinging from a pole than for a boardroom, and a silky tank that made Wes think of the beach.

He gestured her to one of the two guest chairs in front of his desk. Usually he sat next to whoever he was meeting with, making everything more casual, which was how he liked things. But this time, he didn't want casual. He wanted anything but, so he took the chair behind his desk, thinking he needed as much space from this woman as possible.

Kenna sat and crossed her legs.

Since she didn't wear stockings—yes, he'd noticed in spite of himself—the unmistakable sound of skin sliding against skin distracted him for a moment, but only a moment before his boss's voice sounded off in his head.

Take care of my little girl. See if she's as good as I know she can be.

Oh yeah, this was going to be fun. "I'll get right to the point," he said. "I've been acting vice president for nearly a year."

"Let me guess. And you thought you had the job in the bag?"

Hell, yes, he'd thought that. And it was a kick in the teeth to find out differently. "Do you really want to know what I think?"

She leaned back and settled in as if she had all the time in the world. "Oh, yes. I have a feeling it's very interesting."

"All right." He propped his elbows on his desk. "I don't approve of you getting this job simply because of who you're related to. Without any merit."

"Without merit?"

"There are people within this very hotel who resent—"

"You mean you. *You* resent."

"—people who've worked extremely hard to get where they are—"

"And I haven't. Or so you assume." She nodded, then leaned in, too. Steepled her fingers together and spoke over them. "I'm afraid you're just going to have to deal with whatever your hang-ups are about working with me, Mr. Roth, because I'm here now."

"Yes," he agreed tightly. "I am going to have to deal with it. But so will you. We're in the middle of—"

"Renovations. Employee contracts."

So she'd done a little bit of research. He didn't feel overly impressed. "And more. We'll have to learn to deal with this together."

"Sounds like fun."

A headache began at the base of his skull. "Your

father wants us to comanage this place in order to get you the experience you need to move up the ladder at Mallory Enterprises."

She blinked, for one brief flash, clearly startled.

He wasn't touched. "The way I see it, that puts us directly at odds. On the one hand, we need to work together to see that this place shines and makes us both look good. On the other hand, we're competitors for the next rung up on that ladder." Was she even paying attention anymore? It was hard to tell. Her eyes—deep forest green and full of secrets— were right on his, but she seemed preoccupied. "Kenna?"

"Yes?" As if still upset by his spoiled-daughter comment—yeah, right, like her attention span was that long, he'd read her résumé—she ran her tongue over her lower lip, eating off a good amount of her gloss, which, he hadn't noticed before, smelled like peaches and cream.

Much.

"Are you listening?" he asked politely.

"Oh, I'm listening. You think I'm going to try to take your job."

"Actually, no, I'm not worried about you taking my job."

"Well, then, what are you worried about?"

Yeah, what the hell was he worried about? He

only had to share the position he'd always wanted with the boss's daughter, leaving him in the ever-so-unenviable position of having either to make her look good for her father, or make her look bad to further his career. Great. Excellent. And to think he'd thought this whole thing a bad idea.

She came to a slow stand. "I went to business school and—"

"I know your qualifications."

"Then you also know I grew up within this world…"

Yes, he knew. As opposed to his life, which had started in the gutter.

"Not that I ever imagined myself working here since—" She chewed on her lower lip—no longer glossed—and looked at him with an expression he couldn't place.

Mistrust?

She mistrusted *him*?

Now why the hell that got to him, he had no idea. "Since what?"

"Since nothing. Forget it."

He should, but he had to admit, his curiosity had gotten the better of him. Anyone within the company would give their eyeteeth to have this job. There were several qualified people, probably crying in their coffee right this very minute because Mr. Mallory had given it to *him*.

And his daughter.

Wes wasn't worried about the others. He knew he was the best man for the job, just as he knew he'd worked his tail off for it for years. No guilt there.

But if he were Kenna, he'd feel that guilt in spades. She'd done nothing other than go to college—on her daddy's wallet no doubt—and then she'd taken a series of jobs that on paper suggested either a bipolar condition or a serious attention deficit disorder. This vagabond background made her completely unsuitable for the job, and everyone around her would feel the same way. As a manager, that was going to make it inherently difficult on her, and therefore also on him. Surely her father had to know that.

Could she handle it? He actually hadn't heard much about her until recently. The gossip mill suddenly had become agog with rumors, how she'd tricked her father into giving her the job, how she'd stepped all over her cousin—who'd been working at Mallory Enterprises for years—to get placed ahead of her. How all she'd had to do was bat her pretty long lashes and the world bowed at her feet.

Wes had little patience for the gossip, and less patience for the subject of the rumors. In his thirty-three years he'd learned that hard work and dedication would get him where he wanted to be, nothing else, and he expected the same from the people he worked with. So, despite a poor first impression, he would make his own judgment about her.

And stop noticing the peaches-and-cream lip-gloss.

To that effect, he stopped looking at her face, but that was trouble in itself. She was still standing, which left him quite the view, with his eyes just about belly-button level.

Her tank and skirt required sunglasses to look at, but he squinted and braved it. Both hugged her body, emphasizing her mile-long legs, her curves...and the slight outline of a ring at her navel.

Inanely, he wondered what else was pierced.

Oh, man. Bad idea to wonder such things, and he removed his glasses so that she was nothing but a blur.

Much better.

"Well." There was an arctic cold front in her tone. "What should we start with?"

"The best thing would be for you to familiarize yourself with what we're doing."

She nodded in agreement. "I'd like to start with the renovations and the accounting associated with

that. Start preparing the final statements and reports."

"Fine." Good. Let her tackle the tedious task far,
far away from him.

"Where would I find those records?"

"In the records room. Next floor up."

"Great. As much as I've enjoyed your company,
I'm off. I'm sure I'll be seeing you." Her tone was
only slightly warmer than that previous arctic temperature.

When she was gone, Wes let out a slow breath.
Seeing you. He sank back to the chair and wondered
why that had sounded more like a threat than a
promise.

3

KENNA SPENT hours in the records rooms, fascinated by everything. Locked away, alone, absorbing numbers and statements and projections, she actually thought she could enjoy this. Even thrive on it.

By the time she resurfaced, she was shocked to realize the entire day had gone by. Her stomach growled loudly in protest, and she went back to the corporate office level, eager now to jump right into her job.

The reception area was empty. The entire floor was empty. She checked her watch in tune to her still-growling stomach—5:09 p.m. Not that late—

A young man walked by. His name tag said, Intern: Jimmy Owens.

"Jimmy." She gestured him closer. "Where is everyone?"

"Oh, they're gone. Last week there were meetings every night, going really late. Lots of grumblings, you know? Anyway, tonight Mr. Roth sent everyone home at five, including himself, to make up for it. I'm heading out now myself."

Ah. A morale booster and an excellent idea. The only thing that surprised her was that someone like Weston Roth had even thought of it.

She left the building as well and drove around San Diego for a while, reacquainting herself with her childhood town. She drove past Seaport Village, the Horton Plaza, Ocean Beach...Sea World. Her stereo was blasting, her brain racing. Thinking in her old Civic soothed her, as did the sights.

Eventually, she ended up back at the beach, and got out to walk. Nothing beat the feel of the sand between her toes, the pounding of the waves on the shore. It gave her a warm fuzzy just standing there inhaling the salty summer air. College and traveling had been an adventure, but this was home.

She wanted to be here. Wanted to show her family what she could do. Misplaced pride? No doubt. And no doubt she'd pay for it, but she was going to do it anyway.

Sure, things had gotten off to a rocky start, but she was the queen of rocky starts, so that didn't scare her. And sure, people at the San Diego Mallory— more specifically *one* person, Wes himself—had doubts about her abilities and weren't shy about expressing them, but that didn't scare her either. All her life she'd been underestimated, but she knew how to land on her feet.

She could do this. And after today, happily swimming in numbers and reports all day, she actually wanted to do well at this job.

At least for six months.

Bending to grab up a couple of rocks, she hefted one in her hand and skimmed it over the water. It bounced five, six...seven times. A personal record.

A personal record...just like this job would be.

No FAMILY had such torturous family dinners as the Mallorys did on Monday nights, when personal lives were pried open and dissected for mistakes. When career achievements were heralded...and shoved in everyone's face.

Kenna hadn't been to one of her mother's family events in years, and she would have been perfectly happy to miss this one, but now that she was back in town, she was expected. And seeing how she was going to make her father's favorite employee's life hell on earth by just being herself, she felt generous.

Not that she didn't intend to give one hundred percent to the job, because she did. She was going to blow everyone's socks off with her plans and ideas.

Still refreshed from her walk on the beach, she

walked into the Encinitas family mausoleum. Home for the next six months.

They were all in the dining room, a room fit for royalty with all its pomp and splendor, and as she headed there, she automatically slowed down, remembering the days of her childhood.

Don't run, Kenna.

Don't be so wild, Kenna.

Slow down, Kenna.

For God's sake, do you always have to be so exuberant, Kenna?

Why can't you just fit in, Kenna? Okay, no one had really ever asked her that, but she'd heard it just the same. The long traditionally-set table was full of family heirlooms. Over fancy china and crystal, her cousin Serena zinged a set of mental daggers her way. Once upon a time, they'd played with dolls together. Fought over the middle-school football jocks. Smirked over each other's prom dresses.

Being the same age had given them years and years to cultivate their differences, namely that Serena was the perfect Mallory, and Kenna was the wild, unfavorable one. Surprisingly, in recent years, there had been no dissent between them at all. After all, Serena had what she wanted, a job at Mallory Enterprises, and Kenna, the family black sheep, had posed no threat.

Yet now that black sheep had come home, stepped right over Serena on the career ladder, and for that Kenna was actually sorry, even while knowing that if Serena had really been good enough, she'd have Kenna's job by now and her father would never have bothered to call her.

Stepping all the way into the room, she smiled and waved.

Her aunt Regina and uncle Stephan were seated across from Serena, with Kenna's parents at either end of the table like bookends. Everyone was looking at her as if she was something the cat had dragged in.

Except for her mother, of course, who wore the perpetual worried-mother frown. She'd spent years giving Kenna just that exact look.

Oh, joy. Festive evening ahead.

"Hey, gang," she said cheerily, testing the welcome waters.

She got a few muted hellos.

And it occurred to her, right then and there, that to preserve her sanity she was going to need her own space, pronto. Her Santa Barbara apartment was out, she couldn't make the three-and-a-half-hour commute twice a day. But unfortunately, until she actually learned what her salary was and received a paycheck, she was a tad stuck.

No worries though, from her early days of attending college without a trust fund, Kenna had become an expert at micro-managing and budgeting. She'd figure it out. "So..." Kenna plopped herself down and grabbed a fork. "How is everyone?"

Her father would have spoken—probably to blast her for the "honey I'm home" comment at work, but her mother cocked her head and gave him the quelling, calm look. Her mother was always calm, which Kenna supposed was a good trait for a surgeon.

"Sorry I missed you today, Dad. Lots to do."

"Really? Like what?"

"Well, I read up on the renovations, for one."

"Ah, yes. We're just now in the last phase."

"I know. I have to say, I'm not that impressed with the budgeting."

Her father blinked. "You...read the budget?"

"And you actually understood it?" This from Serena.

Kenna shot her a look, then turned back to her father. "Did you know you're spending more money on samples and mock-ups than you do on your employee benefits?"

"Appearances are extremely important, especially when you're dealing with a service. And don't let anyone tell you otherwise. We want this hotel to cater to a certain clientele and—"

"I know, but—"

"Kenna." Serena laughed. "Surely you don't entertain the notion that you're going to jump in and change everything, including the foundation of elegance the company was built upon?"

Her father laughed, so did everyone else.

Except Kenna. She sat and took a deep breath. Truly, it was amazing her cousin's nose wasn't brown.

"So. What else did you read up on?" In true Mallory style her father continued his prodding into her day.

Kenna took a big scoop of potatoes. Carbo loading for the evening ahead. "Financials."

"She was so busy reading, she never met a soul," Serena said, and ate her green beans.

The twig. "I needed to educate myself," Kenna said. She loved her family, and she was fairly certain they loved her, but sometimes she couldn't believe they shared DNA. "I don't like to go mouthing off without the facts."

Serena sent a few more daggers Kenna's way.

"What do you think of Roth?" her father asked Kenna.

"Well..." She took a sip of water and tried to formulate a thought that would be politically correct enough. "He's everything I thought he'd be." That seemed safe enough. She stabbed at her perfectly prepared rare steak.

Serena made a choked noise, and when Kenna looked at her, she lifted her chin. "I'm having trouble picturing the two of you working together."

"Really?" Kenna eyed her cousin, the perfect Mallory with her Katharine Hepburn beauty and elegant style that came from years of being rich. "Why is that?"

"Well..." Serena thought about it as she daintily chewed. "Weston and I were together in the Los Angeles Mallory before we were transferred here, so I feel I'm somewhat of an expert on him. He has an incredible work ethic."

"And I don't?"

"Hey, you're the one who spent six memorable weeks dabbing drool off old men's chin in a retirement home."

"That was a decent job, Serena."

"Sure. You've had lots of decent jobs...about one every six months. Look, all I'm saying is that Wes is stable, smart and greatly admired. Right, Uncle Kenneth?"

Kenna's father nodded proudly.

"Work means everything to him," Serena said. "While you on the other hand—" She stopped to let out a little laugh that assured everyone in the room she wasn't *completely* slamming Kenna, she was simply teasing. "Well, we just established your résumé is a bit...scattered. I mean, combing poodle tails?"

Kenna smiled through the urge to tip a glass of ice water into her cousin's lap. "It's funny, the things you'll do to eat when you don't have a happy, hefty bank account."

Serena had the good grace to back off. Somewhere deep, *deep* down inside, Kenna knew there lurked a good woman, but God knows how far buried she was. Sighing, she pushed her plate away and rose. "You know what? I'm full. What I need is some good sleep before another big day." She kissed her mother's cheek. "Good night."

"Good night," her father said. "I'll wake you at six for a run."

Oh, good Lord. She hadn't seen six in the morning since...ever. She hadn't been under their noses in too many years to go back to checking in, being watched.

Sure, the suggestions would be made kindly enough, but she'd be expected to follow. She'd be given a curfew, complete with random breath tests for alcohol done in the guise of good-night kisses.

No. No way could she do it, even if all she'd planned on drinking tonight was some hot tea. "I just realized," she said gently. "I should be living at the hotel for now. To immerse myself and get a real feel for the place."

Serena's mouth fell open in dismay, most likely because she hadn't thought of it first.

Score: Kenna—1, Serena—0.

4

"I'M STAYING at the hotel," Kenna said into her cell phone as she drove.

"*The* hotel? Can I stay with you?"

Ray was one of her closest friends. He was both a waiter and an actor, but mostly a waiter. And one of the few people who understood and accepted Kenna unconditionally. "I don't think you heard me correctly," she said. "I'm going to be staying in my *father's* hotel."

"So yeah, the atmosphere is bound to be a bit stiff, but baby cakes, the place is amazing. Have you seen the furnishings?"

"Yes, they're overpriced and pretentious."

"You sound a little stressed."

"Just a little," she admitted.

"Because you're not breathing correctly. Remember—"

Kenna mouthed the words with him, rolling her eyes. "No one can stress me out but me. I *know*."

"That's right, sugar. And don't you forget it.

Look, all you have to do is please Dad, right? He'll probably give you back control of your trust fund."

"I don't want a trust fund."

"Baby, sweetie, doll, you were born to own a trust fund."

Kenna laughed. "I've changed."

"Which is exactly the point of this whole thing. You're going to take this job and do it your way. Not theirs, not the conventional, easy way, but your way. Kenna-style. Do it, girl. Show 'em."

"Yeah." She smiled, and this time a deep breath worked. God, she loved this man. "You know I don't even own a pair of stockings."

He laughed, but it was a warm and affectionate one. "With your legs, no stockings required. You'll figure it all out, Kenna. You always do."

Yeah, she'd figure it out. But after she disconnected, her smile faded a little, because in a way she didn't often feel, she was unsure.

Not to mention good and lost. Damn, how had that happened? She should have paid more attention as she'd driven around, but her mind had been elsewhere. Now, she seemed far from the light, open, friendly streets she'd always known. The houses here were small and stacked nearly on top of each other. Peeling paint, barred windows, dead grass and an all-around I-don't-give-a-shit attitude swamped her. Adding insult to injury, her car coughed, then stalled. "Hey," she said and stared at the gauges.

Empty.

With a groan, she drifted to the side of the road and once again picked up her cell phone.

But instead of a dial tone, she received a recorded message. "If you've enjoyed your free phone hours, please call the following one-eight-hundred number to find out just how low a monthly rate you qualify for. Don't be without service for longer than necessary, call now."

"Well, isn't that special." She tossed the useless thing into the back seat with all the rest of the things she'd so hastily shoved in there after vacating her parents' house, then peered out into the summer night. The street was deserted and extremely dark, except for one house.

The sign on the porch read, Teen Zone.

With a sigh, she heaved herself out. Warm, salty air surrounded her as she made her way up the walk.

The teenage girl who answered the door took one look at her and laughed a bit cruelly. "Not a chance, lady. This place is for kids who need a place to go. You're *way* too old."

"No, you don't understand. I just—"

"No offense, but Sarah will just send you to the shelter for hookers. It's down the street and around the corner. Get outta here."

"Tess!" A woman appeared in the doorway beside the teenager. "Sweetie, that's not the way I taught you to answer the door."

The girl hunched her shoulders. "Sorry."

The tall, serene woman, who possibly owned the most calming voice Kenna had ever heard, gave Tess an admonishing look but gently squeezed the girl's hand. "We're here to help, remember? Not judge. Never judge." She held out a hand to Kenna. "I'm Sarah."

Kenna automatically took her hand. It was as warm as her expression and demeanor, and while Kenna appreciated it, she was no charity case. "I'm Kenna. I'm just out of gas. I was wondering if I could use your phone?"

Sarah smiled, and it was a generous one. "Of course. But I've got a five-gallon can in the garage, if you'd rather. I can spare you enough to get where you need to. Come in. Take a load off."

Kenna took in the pitying look, then glanced down at herself, suddenly realizing how she must appear to them. Hair that probably looked as though she'd stuck her finger in a light socket, as it tended to do after a long day. Dress still sans jacket and blatantly sexy, to say the least. Shoes, unquestionably hookerville. So she had a secret slutty side, she couldn't help it. "Look," she said. "I can pay you—"

"No. No, it's okay." Sarah pulled her inside, where a delicious scent engulfed her.

Brownies? Kenna would pay big bucks for brownies.

If she had big bucks.

"As Tess said, this is a teen center for kids who need the escape, but I'd never turn anyone away." Sarah smiled. "Especially a lone woman at night in an area like this one."

Kenna would have laughed, but it might have been a half-hysterical one, so she bit it back. "Honestly. I can pay."

"Okay." Amicably, Sarah led her through a living room that was small and short on furniture, but long on coziness. The walls were a faded yellow, or maybe that was just age. The couch, a well-worn red, had definitely seen its heyday, but looked comfortable enough. There were a bunch of folding chairs and a stack of magazines, as well as a television set with a dial. The seventies revisited all around.

There were several teenagers lounging around

talking or watching a show, each of whom glanced over with a disinterested expression.

Sarah took Kenna to the kitchen, which didn't look any more modern than the living room had. Here the walls were green and the cabinets didn't have fronts. The lovely seventies again. But the brownies on a plate on the scarred Formica table looked new and mouth-watering. Sarah pointed to them. "Would you like one?"

Only more than her next breath, but she didn't want to be any more indebted. "No," she said regretfully. "I need to get going."

Sarah nodded, seeming both serene and sad. "You don't have to, Kenna. No one has to. As Tess said, I could give you the address of a wonderful women's shelter."

"Thank you. You're very kind, but I think you've misunderstood—"

"Just remember we're here." Sarah led her through the back door to the garage for the gas, then walked out front with her. "And I'm always available if you need an ear, or help out of something too big to handle on your own."

"Honestly, I'm not a prostitute. I'm not even on my own, not really. I—" She stopped short at the look on Sarah's face and followed the woman's gaze to her car.

The back of the faded silver Civic was overloaded with the mess she'd made when she'd decided to stay at the hotel. As usual when an idea grabbed her, she'd just acted on it. Without organizing, she'd collected her things, shoving all of it into the back seat. Dresses, shoes, makeup bag, blow dyer, more clothes, more shoes, a stuffed teddy bear from her childhood, you name it, it was back there, overflowing from her suitcases, making it look as though she lived out of the back seat of her car. "This isn't what it looks like. I just—"

"Oh Kenna, you don't ever have to pretend here." Slipping a hand around her waist, Sarah hugged her. "We've all been down on our luck at some point, so just forget about the gas money, okay?"

"No, really. I can pay." Thrilled to be able to do this at least, Kenna reached in for her purse, which unfortunately, was also a big mess, but when she opened her wallet she remembered she hadn't stopped at the bank. Not that there was much in her account at the moment, but—

Sarah put her hand over Kenna's on the wallet. "It's on me."

Kenna looked into the woman's extraordinarily caring eyes and felt a lump clog her throat. "I'll be back," she said rashly. "With money, I promise."

"You don't need money here."

"I want to repay you."

Sarah smiled, a warm, giving, generous one that made Kenna wonder when the last time she herself had given that sort of smile to someone. Well, there'd been that cute guy at TGIF's last week, but other than that...she couldn't remember.

"You could come back and volunteer sometime," Sarah said. "We always need help."

"Okay, sure..." Working at a senior's center was one thing. Volunteering with sullen teens? She'd rather have root-canal surgery. She got into her car, waved when Sarah did, and drove off.

But she couldn't get the place, or Sarah, out of her head. The woman gave kindly to strangers, without strings. So utterly different than the world Kenna was driving to, and unexpectedly, the joy she'd found earlier in the records room of the hotel faded a little.

Sarah's world, riddled with poverty and injustice, suddenly seemed much more like the place for her, a place where she could make a difference, have an impact, put her ideas into action...

But six months was six months, and she'd promised her father.

She just really wished she'd at least taken the offered brownie.

5

WES PLAYED three-on-three basketball every Monday night. They played hard and won hard, and when tonight's game was over, his team was only two victories away from becoming the rec-center league champions.

And two aspirins away from pain relief. He walked to the parking lot with his teammates, each of them trying not to whimper at their various aches and pains. Victors didn't whimper. Men on top of their world didn't whimper.

But, oh God, he wanted to.

"Heading to the pub, Wes?" his buddy, Nick, asked him.

The pub was where they ended up more often than not after a game. There, they either celebrated or commiserated, depending on how the game had gone.

Tonight, there'd be a lot of celebrating, and for a moment, he was tempted. But duty called so he shook his head. "I have to head back to the office."

This was accompanied by boos and hisses, but as his teammates Nick and Steve were a doctor and an attorney respectively, who both put in even more hours than he did, he laughed them off.

He drove to the hotel and parked in his designated spot, noting the one next to him had a freshly painted sign that read Ms. Kenna Mallory. At least it was vacant.

The corporate floors were deserted. He'd given everyone the night off, including himself, but now that the hard play was over and some of his aggressions had been released, he wanted to get some work done. Especially since he'd spent most of the day soothing hurt egos and ruffled feathers. People resented the intrusion of Kenna Mallory at such a high level.

Serena had been the most upset, a situation that gave him mixed feelings. She was a junior conference manager, and reported directly to him, and though she was decent at her job, he'd always felt she had more ambition than actual skill. Given the way she'd gone on and on today, she'd forgotten that she, too, had once been given her job because of her last name. No entry-level positions for Mallory family members.

Either way, he hoped she'd gotten all her whining

and pouting out of her system, because when Serena was on a rant, everyone around her paid.

He sank to his desk and dug in. He loved his work, but he loved his time off as well, and wanted to make sure he got some this weekend, since he actually had a date and was looking forward to a few hours of mindless fun. He looked forward to everything he did these days, because though it had been years since he'd struggled to make something of himself, he'd never forgotten his humble beginnings.

With his current salary several times over what he needed, he was able to do pretty much whatever he wanted. Since he wasn't a frivolous man or one who needed luxuries, this mostly involved extreme sports or spoiling his family when they let him— buying his parents a house, sending them on vacations they'd never dreamed they'd be able to take, getting his brother through college—

A blur of creamy skin, blond hair and an unforgettable fuchsia skirt passed his opened office door. He glanced at his watch. Ten o'clock.

What the hell?

Standing, he rounded his desk to peek out, but yep, it was indeed Kenna Mallory's very fine backside wriggling its way down the hallway, her bare feet in those strappy little sandals that seemed suicidal to him.

"So you're not just a nightmare," he called out, half hoping she'd vanish.

Slowly she stopped, then pivoted to face him, her arms full of a variety of bags, all of which were overflowing with what looked like...stuff. Even as he watched, the blow dryer she'd slung over her shoulder started to slip. "It's not late enough for nightmares."

"What are you doing here?"

"Maybe you missed the Mallory part of the San Diego Mallory."

"I meant," he said dryly, "what are you doing in the offices this late?"

"I wanted to grab some nighttime reading material before checking in—" She broke off to growl in frustration as things started tumbling from her arms.

Wes scooped up the bag, but not in time to keep it from spilling out a magazine, a lipstick case, a styling comb, a compact mirror, a tube of mascara and two tampons.

Hunkering down to help, he deliberately avoided touching the tampons and scooped up the magazine instead. *Outside.* This city girl read an adventure magazine? "I wouldn't have pegged you for an *Out-'side* kind of girl."

"You couldn't peg me for anything—" she snatched it back "—as you don't know the first thing about me. And there happens to be a great article this month on relaxing beach vacations," she relented. "If that matters to you."

Unfortunately just about everything relating to her was going to matter to him, since they were likely going to be joined at the hip for a while, until some other more appealing job came along and she fluttered off.

On her knees, she started gathering things, tossing them back into the bag. "And anyway, at least until we establish some sort of routine...one that'll keep us from killing each other—" she pointed at him with the article in her hand, a tampon "—just get used to seeing me around." She stopped and stared at the tampon, then glared at him as if it was his fault she was using it like a pointer.

"What makes you think we're going to kill each other?" he asked curiously.

She laughed. "Are you saying you're welcoming me with open arms?"

"I plan on welcoming you as I would any employee."

"Well, isn't that a politically correct answer."

"Look, Ms. Mallory—"

"Kenna. My name is Kenna."

"Kenna." He picked up some of her loose change and handed it to her. "I think we can do this in a friendly manner."

"What? Vie for the next rung on the ladder?"

Okay, he probably deserved that. Maybe he'd been a bit stiff earlier. "I'm just saying we're stuck in this position together, and—"

"I'm not stuck. I'm never stuck. I do as I please, when I please, and working here pleases me."

"For the moment."

She froze in the act of stretching for a rogue pen, her skirt rising incredibly high on a tanned, toned thigh, reminding him that she didn't favor stockings. And being the weak male that he was, he wondered if her panties were as bright as the rest of her clothes. Like he needed to know that information.

"Look," she said. "I'm taking this job seriously. So do me a favor and take me seriously. Oh, and by the way, I'm...moving in."

When the words sank in, he raised his gaze to meet her unhappy one. "What?"

"I'm going to be staying here. At the hotel."

Wes didn't often find himself rendered speechless, but somehow he wasn't surprised to find Kenna the woman to do it. "*Why?*"

"Because that also pleases me." She paused then muttered under her breath, "and it's the lesser of two evils."

"Your father said you had to, right?"

"Of course not."

"What did he do, threaten to cut off your credit card?"

If he'd been any closer, her look would have fried him on the spot. "I don't care about his money."

"What *do* you care about?" he asked.

"Not his money," she repeated. "I earn my own. As for what I do care about...I care about my life. Living it how I want to, which until now has been very different than this structured, cutthroat business atmosphere. How about you, Mr. Roth?"

"Wes."

"Wes," she said with an acknowledging bow of her head. "What is it you care about?"

"This structured, cutthroat business, for one."

She actually laughed and reached for the last item on the floor, a lipstick, and put it back into the bag. "Well, that's going to make us quite the interesting pair."

"Yes. Yes, it is." His gaze met hers, and...held. Humor still swam in her eyes, humor and intelligence and an easy love of life.

Damn if that wasn't suddenly, startlingly,

abruptly attractive. He stood. Backed way up, giving her room.

Giving *himself* room.

"I can do this job," she said softly. "I'm good at fiscal planning. Marketing strategies. Structuring business goals. Budgeting, including the remaining renovations, growth...all of it. The one thing I'm not good at is dealing with people who make assumptions about the outer package..." She tossed her blond hair and straightened her stripper's body. "Don't mistake the outer package, Wes."

"How about I won't if you won't?"

"What?"

He pushed up his glasses. "Are you going to deny you took one look at me and lumped me in with every other suit in the building, which, apparently, leaves a bad taste in your mouth?"

"Not a bad taste necessarily."

"Then a bad attitude."

She laughed again, and it was an amazing laugh, a contagious one. "Okay, you got me. I lumped you in with all the dark conservative suits. Just tell me this...what's wrong with color, Wes? Why don't any of you wear any color for God's sake?"

He looked down at his black basketball shorts, black basketball shoes and black T-shirt.

She laughed again. "You never even noticed that's the only color around here, did you?"

"No," he said truthfully, and had to shake his head. "I swear I own a few things that aren't black."

"Yeah? Prove it. Shock me tomorrow. And tightie whities don't count."

He blinked.

"Underwear," she explained. "Plain white Jockey shorts don't count as color."

"I don't wear plain white Jockey shorts."

He wore plain white knit *boxers*, because a guy had to have room.

"Whatever you say."

She was most definitely baiting him, but he absolutely was not going to get into a discussion about underwear. Not at ten o'clock at night, on an empty floor, with no one around save this laughing, sharp-tongued and shockingly attractive woman staring at him.

No way.

She stood up. "So...how about this? I overlook the fact that you look like a Mallory clone, and you overlook the fact that I might appear better suited for wet T-shirt contests than board-room discussions."

He thought about that. First the wet T-shirt—he couldn't help that—then her proposal.

She waited for a moment, then said, "Come on. I think that's an excellent second compromise, if I do say so myself."

He felt his mouth curve in a smile, his first genuine smile when it came to Kenna. "Deal."

"Deal," she repeated and, gathering her things, walked away. "'Night," she called over her shoulder. "Sleep tight."

Sleep tight. He had a feeling he wouldn't be sleeping tight at all, not for a long time to come.

6

THAT NIGHT, Kenna stayed up late, working in her fancy hotel room. From her little foray into the records department, she'd discovered something interesting. The projected analysis on the renovations, salaries, expenses, everything, had been carefully filled out, and yet there'd been no follow-up since adding this hotel to the Mallory fleet. Because of that, no one could see at a glance how things had gone.

Had they overspent on the renovations done so far? Underspent? What? No way to tell.

Employee contracts were up for renewal, but how could management go into negotiations without seeing how the last contracts had benefited them and *not* benefited them?

So she spent the next two hours burning the midnight oil, working on her little laptop that kept freezing up—the poor thing was so old it could scarcely handle the spreadsheets and reports—

working until she came up with articulate and concise thoughts on the matter.

Only then did she get into bed, satisfied that for one day at least, she'd earned her keep.

But one thing Kenna had never been able to do was turn off her brain. She lay there in her frou-frou room with the antique Queen Anne bed, staring at the ornately decorated ceiling painted in elegant cream and thought about what she'd done.

Committed to six months in this place.

Sure, the numbers and accounting would be fun, and so would torturing Serena with her presence, and maybe even a little torture thrown Wes's way as well, but no doubt, being here would also take its toll.

Although Wes had actually, genuinely made her laugh tonight. Shocking. She'd always had a thing for a guy who could make her laugh, and she had a sinking feeling that beneath Weston Roth's fancy dark suits beat the heart of a sharp cynic.

Call her sick, but she liked that, too.

Okay, forget sleep. It just wasn't going to happen. Tossing aside her covers, she looked around, wondering how to amuse herself. For the first time in recent memory she actually had luxury at her fingertips and she was just lying around. What a complete waste of her time.

She drew herself a bubble bath in the decadent bathtub. Sinking into the hot water was heaven, and she lay back, wondering what tomorrow would bring, if people would appreciate her report...

And if Wes was going to wear a color tomorrow.

When she finally tried sleep again, slightly more relaxed now, she fell quickly. Unfortunately, somewhere near dawn, or what felt like it, the phone rang.

"Okay, listen up, cousin," Serena said when Kenna managed to get the phone to her ear. "We have a few things to discuss."

She blinked at the clock. Eight. In the morning. "Oh God." She leapt out of bed. "I'm late."

"Well, duh."

"I didn't want to be late." She grabbed up the clock radio, which indeed had been set for the proper time, and had indeed gone off, and was at this very moment spilling out soft-rock music.

Too soft-rock, apparently, as it hadn't come close to waking her. She tossed the thing down and looked around. Clothes. She needed clothes.

"Look, cuz, stay on page with me now. This call is about *moi*. Okay? So listen up. Stay away from him, he's mine."

Kenna eyed a skirt hanging off the back of a chair

that probably had seen the eighteenth century. "Stay away from who?"

"Don't be coy. Wes has the best ass ever. He's a catch and I already have the catcher's glove on."

"Weston *Roth?*"

"*Wake up*, would you? Slap yourself, pinch yourself, something."

"I am awake." Now, anyway. What to go with the skirt? "You make him sound like a piece of meat."

"Do I?"

Kenna stopped in the act of stripping. "You're serious. You're going after him because he's got a great ass."

"Why else?"

Um, because he was smart. Because he had a job.

Okay, because he had a great ass.

But a good ass did not a good man make. Kenna required far more. Her cousin could have him. "How does he feel about this?"

"Oh, please." Serena scoffed. "If you'd thought of it first, you'd use him, too."

"I have no desire to use him. Or anyone."

"God, you are so sanctimonious, you know that? I know damn well—hell, the entire family knows damn well—you have this little secret fantasy of fitting in, of being like the rest of us. Now that chance is being dangled out in front of you like a carrot with this job, so don't pretend you don't care. You want Uncle Kenneth to see you, to see the real you, and be proud of that woman. And if Wes turns out to be able to help you with that, you'll use him in a heartbeat. So. I'm telling you now. Back off."

"You're insane."

"Fine. You don't want to back off. Then may the best woman win."

"I'm not going to play that game with you, Serena."

"Whatever you say. But he's going to be mine. Good luck today, cuz. Ta-ta."

When the dial tone rang in her ear, Kenna hung up and shook her head. Good luck? She was going to need it, but not for the reasons Serena thought. Yes, Wes was way too into Mallory Enterprises and all it entailed, but he was entitled to be the man he wanted to be, just as she was entitled to be herself.

This wasn't personal. She wouldn't use him, not to fit in, not to do her job, not for anything.

She was going to do this on her own.

Hence the need for good luck.

Hopping around, she shoved her legs one at a time into her skirt, imagining Wes checking his fancy watch. Well, at least she didn't have to take the time to make her bed, she actually had maid service for that. Her heels were lower today, but not by much, as exceptional height gave her confidence. Her skirt was longer, too, but tighter, making long strides difficult if not a detriment to her health. The blouse, however, she prided herself on. It wasn't exactly business-like with its sheerness, but the camisole beneath was a definite antique, and soft and creamy against her skin. In the ensemble she felt pretty and sexy, and when she was pretty and sexy she knew she could take on the world.

So world, here she came.

She left her room and got on the elevator, where she watched the glowing numbers descend, until she stepped off on the corporate floor, which opened into a large, fancy reception area decorated as the rest of the hotel was—sophisticated and refined.

The air buzzed with activity. Everywhere she looked, well-dressed, *darkly* dressed employees went about their day doing...actually, she still wasn't clear on that part because she hadn't studied the organizational charts and job descriptions yet. But she would be.

Her cousin Serena, looking extremely Mallory in her perfectly fitted navy-blue business suit, stood next to one of the front desks. It was occupied by a man in his early twenties whipping his fingers across a keyboard.

"So what, you're swamped," Serena said to him, practically hanging over his shoulder. "This is your job, Josh, and my uncle—"

"Yeah, yeah, we all know who the uncle is." He shot her an annoyed look. "Now, if you'd quit downloading porn from the Internet, maybe you'll stop freezing your computer up."

"It's not porn. All I wanted was that firefighter calendar."

"How can you tell they're firefighters?" Josh clicked a few keys and a full body shot of an almost-naked hunk filled the screen. "The only equipment he's got is his—"

"Just fix it, computer boy."

"Right." Josh's tie was loose, his sleeves shoved past his elbows. With his lean body, hunching shoulders and frowning features, he looked quite tense but then Serena tended to do that to a person.

"What is it with firefighters anyway?" he muttered. "I could look that good in suspenders, no shirt and a fire hat, too. Want to see it?"

"Not in this lifetime," Serena said, then she caught sight of Kenna and affixed a superior smile to her mouth. "Well, look who decided to show up for work. Uncle Kenneth told me to make you right at home in a special office, so I picked one out, just for you." The smile she sent Kenna put her on full alert. "Last one on the left. You've got meetings all day, starting..." She checked her diamond-studded watch. "Oops. Ten minutes ago. The first one is a meet-and-greet in Conference Room A. Come on, I'd better take you."

"I can find it."

"Probably, but it'll be far more fun to watch you muddle your way through your first real job."

"You're so incredibly sweet first thing in the morning," Kenna said. "It's touching." They moved down yet another fancy hall with marble floors that made her wonder how her father kept from being sued right and left with broken ankles incurred by walking on the high-gloss surfaces.

Serena opened a set of floor-to-ceiling double doors with an extremely smug expression on her face. The room had a table larger than the apartment Kenna had left in Santa Barbara, and the chairs surrounding it were filled.

Wes came toward her with a smile on his face that didn't meet his eyes behind his glasses. She wondered if he'd forgotten to eat his Cheerios for breakfast but didn't have time to ask him before he started introducing her to staff—marketing director, sales director, customer service director—you name it, she met them.

"So, tell us, Kenna." Serena gave her a sweet

smile after the intros. "How do you intend to make your mark here?"

Kenna looked around in surprise. Everyone looked at her right back.

Including Wes, who raised a challenging brow that made her want to smack him. She lifted the reports she'd worked on in the middle of the night. "Well, I plan on taking an interest in how our projected budgets line up with the finished projects outcome. I noticed that on the renovations, for instance, we've gone way over—"

"Honestly, Kenna." Serena's laugh tinkled throughout the room. "You'll have enough to do in the present without worrying about the past."

"The past is quite important to any corporation's present or future." Kenna looked around her, but oddly enough, few met her gaze.

Except Wes. He cocked his head and studied her, the only one in the room to do so directly. "You have paperwork to back up your thoughts?"

Did she have paperwork? She loved paperwork. "Yep."

"It sounds extremely interesting."

"It is extremely interesting."

He wiggled his fingers toward her. "May I?"

Kenna looked around again. Suddenly everyone

was meeting her gaze. What a bunch of suck-ups. "Sure." She tossed him the reports.

He caught them with ease, tucked them under his arm and looked around him. "Thanks. Okay, people, here's how the VP positions are going to work." He then outlined how the division of duties would affect them, and what it meant to each department, while Kenna used the time to take stock of the fact that dark conservative clothing prevailed.

Except for Wes and his red tie, that is. She nearly grinned at that. Besides the tie, her turquoise skirt was the bright spot in the room.

When he finished, she shook a lot more hands. There was Mr. Bad Tie, Ms. Needs Highlights and so many others she hoped like hell she remembered their names later. In the midst of the can't-wait-to-work-with-you speeches, Kenna caught Serena's go-to-hell expression. Kenna knew from past experience that Serena was officially out to make her life miserable. Great. Just what she needed. Kenna escaped as soon as possible, looking forward to finding her office and digging into more work. On the way out, she grabbed Serena's arm. "Which office did you say was mine?"

An unholy gleam came into her cousin's eyes. "Fifth one on the right past the desk you saw me at earlier. Later."

Yeah. Hopefully not.

Kenna followed the directions, counting the doors, and had just put her hand on the handle when she heard someone clear their throat.

Already she knew that sound, as the man it belonged to was a bundle of contradictions—cool and aloof, and yet capable of unpredictable bouts of quick wit and good humor. She'd told herself to ignore him, but deciding it and doing it were two entirely separate things.

Slowly she pivoted and faced one most definitely not-ignorable Weston Roth.

His smile was pure trouble. "Next round," he said, and lifted a stack of papers and files in his hand. "These are for you."

7

KENNA STARED at Wes and took a deep breath. Next round. Perfectly chosen words. Fighting words. And Wes certainly had the build of a finely honed boxer, all tall and toughly lean.

Oh, yes, this was the next round. Bring it on. "What do you have there?"

"Since you gave me your paperwork, I thought it only fair to share mine for the day. I've got a stack of files and reports that will bring you up to speed for the week's worth of meetings."

She stared at him, she couldn't help it. He was actually going to bring her into the decision-making process. He was going to treat her like an equal.

She'd known he'd have to make at least a pretense of it, but it appeared he planned on doing more than that. Why that touched her, she had no idea, but it did. It touched her and took her completely off guard. Clearly she'd been feeling a little more vulnerable than she could have imagined. But she hadn't gone with the waterproof mascara this morning so she bucked up. Besides, it was one thing to have a bad or weak moment, another entirely to show it.

"In particular," he said. "I've got employee contracts and union demands. We're meeting with the reps in an hour to discuss strategies, so you might want to hustle."

The lump turned to pure irritation. *An hour?* She could never—

"Can you get it together?"

"Of course," she said, her nose so high in the air she risked a nosebleed.

Wes gestured to her still-closed office. "Did you pick this one?"

"Serena did."

His dark-blue eyes, deep and mysterious behind his glasses, gave nothing away, nothing except a small glimmer of amusement. "You two are close then, huh?"

"Like this." She lifted two fingers, entwined. "So...we're working on employee contracts today."

"Just this morning. By eleven we'll be going over the financial statements. Quarterlies just came in."

Great, she'd be in her element, as opposed to this morning and the union work, which she knew nothing about. Yikes. She'd have to speed-read, she'd have to— Her thoughts scattered away when she realized he was staring at her. Specifically, her mouth. "Um...what? Do I have crumbs on my face or something?"

"Nothing." He looked away.

And she found herself looking at *his* mouth. Firm and...well, downright sexy if she was being honest.

Whoa. She had no idea where that completely inappropriate thought had come from. He was a suit. He was a Mallory drone. He was completely and totally not for her.

Ever.

"Okay, listen." He took a step closer, pinning her with nothing more than his sharp eyes and the feel of his big, beautiful body nearly brushing hers. "Did something weird just happen?"

"No." She shook her head. "Absolutely not."

He looked at her for a long moment. "You're right. It was nothing."

She managed a smile. "Look at that, our third agreement. This is going to be a piece of cake."

His mouth curved. "Cake, huh?"

Oh, boy, he had a smile. It went straight to her good spots, which hello, hadn't been heard from in a while. It made her own smile freeze.

"Don't do that," he said quietly. "Don't overthink it. It was nothing. Remember that."

"And even if it wasn't nothing, I'm good at discipline. I can eat just one cookie or even one chip and resist—"

"I'm not a cookie, Kenna. Or a chip."

She couldn't help it, she laughed, thinking a cookie and a delicious-looking man weren't really all that different.

"Terrific." He let out a frustrated breath. "Look, I don't suppose you can *not* laugh? Ever?"

Slowly, fighting a smile, she shook her head.

"Yeah." A muscle in his jaw ticked.

Interesting. Also a little unsettling. She tugged his red tie. "Was this for me, Wes?"

His dark, dark eyes were inscrutable as they roamed her face. "Maybe I just needed a splash of color." He leaned past her and opened the door.

Of course he smelled fantastic. And she had to work not to snuggle in and breathe deep of his woodsy scent. Oh brother, what was the matter with her today? Had it been that long since a man had looked at her?

Yes, she had to admit. Her last boyfriend had taught yoga and had been so low-key, so relaxed, she'd often put a hand over his mouth and nose in bed to make sure he was still breathing.

He hadn't even realized when she'd left him.

He probably still hadn't realized.

To distance herself, she walked into her new office, if it could be called an office. The place was spotless, she'd give it that. And smaller than a postage stamp. Seriously, the place was too small to be a closet. The chrome desk took up the entire floor, so much so that when two women and a man tried to follow them in—Ms. Needs Highlights, Mr. Bad Tie and a woman Kenna hadn't met—each with their arms full of various files and computer reports, they had to crowd in the doorway rather than come in.

"Ms. Mallory, here's the conferencing schedule for the week—"

"Ms. Mallory, I've got subcontractor contracts for you to go over—"

"Ms. Mallory, I have—"

Head spinning, Kenna held up a hand. She looked around the place and shook her head. Serena had definitely gotten her.

New score: Serena—1, Kenna—1.

Wes stepped up. "I'll talk to Serena—"

"No," she said firmly, not wanting to give Serena any extra reasons to deal with Wes. That alone made so little sense, she shook the thought off. "I'll handle it." With a deep breath, she looked at the employees waiting to hand her stacks of...stuff. She'd had classes in both management and hotel management, she'd grown up on bedtime stories about the hotel industry, but for the first time it truly hit her that she had no practical experience. The urge to panic nearly overcame her. *Calming images,* she could hear Ray telling her. Calming images. *She was in a boat, on a beautiful ocean bay...*

With a leak. "Lay it on me," she said, and held out her hands.

In less than sixty seconds, they'd left her a mountain of paperwork and had vanished.

She looked at Wes.

He looked at her. "You should know, I told them to bring you those files."

"Did you think it would make me run for the hills?"

He looked her over. "Are you feeling the urge to run?"

"Hell, no." She fingered the files. "And I should tell you, I'm not feeling scared either."

"What are you feeling?"

"Very, very competitive." She smiled. "I'm going to do this, Wes."

"So you've said."

"I'm sorry if you thought this job would be yours alone, but I'm not sorry I'm here."

Before he could respond to that, her phone started ringing.

"I don't think an assistant has been assigned to you yet." Wes reached for the phone.

She pushed his hand aside and got it herself. "Kenna Mallory," she answered, but the phone kept ringing. She realized her phone had three lines and each of them were going off. She listened to some harassed duty manager start to ramble on about a celebrity wanting to redecorate her suite with her own artwork.

"Can you hold?" Kenna clicked on to the other line and was rewarded with a housekeeping manager ranting about the scheduling mix-up and how she needed authorization to call in off-duty help. "Hold please."

By the time she got to line three, the person had either hung up or been transferred to depths unknown.

"What do you have?" Wes asked.

"Nothing I can't handle." She looked pointedly toward the door.

"Oh, you want to be on your own."

"I do pretty good on my own." She punched line one. "Hello. Tell the celebrity she can bring in any artwork she'd like as long as she doesn't mar the walls or damage any artwork currently in her room." She punched line two. "Call in whatever help you need to get through the shift." She hung up the phone and looked at Wes.

"The celebrity should have been told no," he said.

"Maybe he or she has been on tour and is home-sick, and needs a piece of home," she said.

"Maybe they're just spoiled rotten."

"We're here to serve, Wes."

"Is that why you approved the extra staff? Which, by the way, will cost time and a half."

"The employees will love it, so it'll help out both the service for the day, and boost morale at the same time."

He stared at her, then shook his head.

"What?"

"You're nothing like your father."

And you're just like him, she thought.

He took one last look around. "This office is too small for you."

"It's fine—"

"Serena's is twice the size of this one."

"Yes, well, size means a lot to Serena."

"I would have thought it meant a lot to you, too."

His gaze was daring, and she'd never been good at resisting a baiting. "Well, now," she drawled and lifted a shoulder. "That depends on what we're siz-ing."

He undoubtedly would have responded to that if his pager hadn't gone off. He looked down at the thing hooked on his hip, then looked at her. "They're here. The union reps."

"Okay." Calming images. She could do this. She picked up the correct files. "Should I speed-read here or are you going to give me the Cliff Notes version?"

He let out a grudging smile.

Oh man, she'd nearly forgotten how attractive he could be when he did that, grudging or otherwise. "You think this is amusing?"

"No, actually," he said. "I'm quite intrigued by your coolness under pressure. You've got the blond bombshell look down, and yet..."

"And yet?"

"You're the one of the toughest woman I've met."

She opened her mouth, ready to leap down his throat, but she was certain that there'd been a compliment in there somewhere. "Thanks. I think."

"You're welcome. I think."

8

WES BRIEFED her on the way to the union meeting in short, concise sentences that were actually quite helpful. Not once was his tone condescending or critical, though she imagined behind his glasses simmered resentment at having to help her out in the first place.

The man was clearly conflicted on this sharing-the-job thing.

That made two of them.

The actual meeting went well, until she realized she sided with the union and not the hotel. At one point, she turned to Wes to help explain what it was the union wanted and why it was such a good thing, but the look on his face stopped her cold.

Oops. Wrong side.

Afterward, she avoided Wes and the fallout that was coming, instead making her way through the hotel and stepping outside for some fresh air. She sat on a marble bench in a fabulously lush garden overlooking the ocean and wished she could take a nap on the beach.

"How do you think it went?"

She looked up at Wes, who looked just as at home outside in the California sun as he did in the board room. "Is that a trick question?"

"Of course not," he said.

"And you'd like the truth?"

"Yes."

"I think you did exceptionally well for the hotel."

He frowned. "What does that mean?"

"It means good for you, you saved my father tons of money."

"But...? I'm quite positive I heard a *but* at the end of that sentence."

"But..." She looked at the glorious summer sky. "I think you did a crappy job for your employees. You didn't back down on the two percent difference in salary increase they wanted, nor the onsite day-care...not even on the issue of sick days needing to be increased. All in all, the union accepted a sucky package, because you wined and dined their rep into thinking he got a great deal."

"Well, don't hold back," he said wryly. "Tell me how you really feel."

"I always will, Wes."

He looked at her for a long moment and sighed. "Somehow, I'm sure that's going to be more a curse than a blessing."

THE NEXT MORNING Kenna had just arrived in her office—at eight o'clock sharp, amazingly enough—when Wes appeared in her doorway.

"Next round?" she guessed.

"I read your report on the renovations, regarding the progress we've made—or not, in this case—staying on budget."

It shouldn't have given her a little thrill, that he'd read her work. "Did you?"

"And the thing is, a lot of the plans changed in progress. Your father upped the amount of art he wanted purchased, for example, as well as increasing the number of antiques in each room. Those two things alone added considerable cost, and he didn't seem to mind."

"It seems frivolous, given our other policies."

"Such as?"

"Such as no price breaks for locals. No specials in the restaurants. No package deals—"

"How does that relate to the art purchasing?"

"I'm just saying, we're overcharging our local residents simply because someone wanted an extra picture on the wall, a picture that cost more than a small fortune. It doesn't make any sense."

"We're not catering to the locals."

"That's awfully snobbish."

"Kenna." He laughed. Shook his head. "Have you looked at this place? By its very nature, it's snobbish."

Before she could answer, a woman came to the door. Kenna recognized her as Carrie, one of the security managers.

"Our new equipment has arrived," she said.

"New equipment?" Kenna asked.

"We ordered all new security cameras, radios and such. The latest in hotel technology," Wes explained. "It's been back-ordered for months. The employees have all been to classes and training, and they can't wait to dig in."

"Thought you'd want to look over the inventory first," Carrie said. "Before I alert the rest of security."

"I do, thanks."

"I do, too." Kenna smiled into Wes's face, which had a priceless expression of bewilderment and vexation. He'd have liked to do this alone.

Too bad. He moved to the door and so did Kenna, meaning there was a lot of full-body contact as they squeezed through the narrow opening.

"Kenna—"

"*Wes*—" Pretending that being plastered against

him in the doorway had absolutely no effect on her, when oddly enough, it did, she set a hand on his arm and imitated his warning tone. Beneath her fingers, his muscles were smooth and hard, his skin warm. This close, he seemed even larger, and oddly, not so much intimating as...

Yikes.

Just a little...sexy.

She pulled her hand back.

His gaze remained on hers. "Are you coming with me to get out of reading all those reports on your desk?"

"Absolutely."

Again his lips quirked. He was going to have to stop doing that, because watching them move like that made her wonder what else his lips did well.

Oh boy. Time to go.

"Fine," he said. "We'll go together."

"Fine."

"In the name of orientation."

Whatever he wanted to call it, as long as she got her way.

WES NODDED to employees here and there, as he and Kenna made their way to security, but, despite all the distractions, he found himself watching Kenna walk.

And it was quite a walk. Every step of the way, down the long hallway, then out into the reception area, down the elevator, over priceless carpets and past impressive paintings, through the huge glass doors into the early dazzling San Diego summer sun and onto the patio decking, he watched.

While telling himself he shouldn't.

"Beautiful day," she said when they went through a courtyard, beyond which came the scent of chlorine. The security rooms were just beyond the pool area. "I'd still prefer the beach, though. Give me the hot sand and pounding surf any day over the scent of pool."

He lifted his eyes off her legs, which were revealed by the long slit in the skirt with every step she took. Did she know her hips swung to and fro in the most hypnotic way? That she was highly entertaining in a way he couldn't explain, and he didn't want to miss anything? He shook his head to clear it. "The beach. Yeah, I was there at the crack of dawn, and it was something."

"What were you doing? Running?"

"Surfing."

She glanced at him over her shoulder. "*You* surf?"

"Is that so strange?"

She laughed. "I'm just trying to picture you without the tie."

"Who says I surf without it?"

She stared at him, then laughed again. "You're very different than I thought you'd be, Weston Roth."

And so was she. They moved close together to make their way through a narrow walkway. Strands of her long blond hair seemed to catch him, tug at him. Annoying as hell.

Worse, she'd dressed like some movie star out of the 1930s. Who could have guessed a long-sleeved blouse and long, long skirt could be so sexy? It might have been the fact that the blouse was sheer, showing a peek-a-boo hint of something lacy beneath.

They came to the pool. Because it was early yet, no one was in the water. Two little girls, wearing matching pink polka-dot bathing suits and inflatable arm rings stood near the edge, screeching at each other.

"Mom said!"

"No, she didn't!" The left one added a shove to the screech.

Her sister shoved back.

Kenna stepped forward. "Hey, there's no lifeguard on duty. Where's your mother?"

The girls paid her no attention. Wes watched them screeching and shoving, and wondered if all little children were devils incarnate. These two especially, as with each push, they brought each other closer to the edge of the pool.

His fearless new partner stepped close, right on the very edge of the tile herself.

He stepped close, too, and tried to warn her. "Uh...Kenna? Bad idea—"

"Where are the pool employees? These girls can't be out here alone." Stepping between the kids, she bent down to their level. "Where's your mom?" she repeated.

"Mom said!" the one on the right said again at an incredible decibel level.

"No, she didn't!" The one on the left reached around Kenna and added another push.

Wes winced. "Kenna—"

With absolute irritation, she whirled on him. "I just need a minute, Wes. Can you give me that?"

He looked down at the edge of the pool, almost directly beneath her feet, and then into her fierce eyes.

Swallowing the dire warning he'd been about to offer, he stood back, calculated the splash level, and then stepped back another few feet. "You know what?" he said. "Take all the minutes you want."

"Thank you." Kenna turned back to the children. "Now," she said, with the patience of a harassed teacher on a Friday afternoon. "I want the two of you to— *Hey!*"

One of the little girls stopped pushing her sister and pushed Kenna.

"Stop that," she said sternly.

The other sister apparently liked this new target, too, and joined in the action, adding her weight to the pushing match.

And that's when it all went bad.

Arms flailing, Kenna flew backward.

Right into the pool.

9

SURFACING, Kenna blew her soggy hair out of her face. Furious, and more than a little embarrassed, she glared at her target. Not the two horrified children, but Weston Roth. "Don't even think about laughing."

"I wouldn't dare."

The two girls, crying now, ran for their mother, who'd just come onto the deck with an armful of towels.

Nice of her to show up.

Kenna's teeth started to chatter, because the contrast between the air temperature and the water temperature was so great and she swam for the side of the pool. That's when it hit her that Wes stood a good ten feet back.

Of course he did, the jerk.

"I could be drowning, you know." She shoved more of her soggy hair from her face. She really was going to have to go with waterproof mascara.

The irritating man merely smiled, though he did step a bit closer. "Are you?"

"*Yes.*"

He laughed, and the low rough sound of his good humor really fried her. She knew damn well he wouldn't be laughing if it was *him* in the water.

"You're talking too much to be drowning," he said, then hunkered down at the edge of the pool, careful to keep his shoes dry. "You're a mess."

"It's very sweet of you to point that out." She lifted a hand, too irritated to swim to the shallow end or toward the ladder. "Pull me out."

Mockingly apologetic, he shook his head. "You said you were going to handle this." His smile was slow, sympathetic and utterly, infuriatingly sexy. "You said—"

"Oh, shut up." She held on to the side of the pool, the water dragging her clothes down while she plotted her revenge, never mind that it was her own stupidity that had landed her in the pool in the first place. Somehow this was his fault, she just knew it. "Give me a h-hand."

She hadn't faked the shiver at the end, but she realized when he frowned in concern that it was a nice touch and immediately added another.

He held out a hand, which she took. And latched

on. Feet braced on the side of the pool, she tugged as hard as she could.

The splash he made after he flew over her head and hit the water was quite satisfactory.

When he broke the surface, he shook his head and stared at her, shocked. "You pulled me in."

She smiled. "Your glasses are crooked." She moved to haul herself out, meaning to do so gracefully, with dignity, so as to fully savor having the last word.

But her clothes weighed a ton. She'd lost one heel, and she couldn't hike her leg up in her tight skirt. "Um...Wes?"

He swam to the edge, with a fine stroke she couldn't help but notice, and shot daggers at her. "What?"

"Could you give me another hand?"

"Hell, no."

She shivered again—not quite a fake one this time—and he rolled his eyes. "Oh, *fine*."

In the next breath, he'd hauled her toward him, and since he could stand, he slipped one large hand around her waist, another other under her legs. His fingers curled just beneath her breast, his strong, warm forearm banding around her upper thighs.

For one all too brief second, she was plastered against his hard chest before he lifted her up and out, unceremoniously depositing her in a growing puddle on the edge of the pool.

At the feet of five gaping employees, all trying not to be amused by this situation. Nice of *them* to show up, too. Someone tossed her a towel.

"Thanks," she said, pulling her clinging clothes away from her body in vain. Giving up, she worked on her hair. "Thanks so much for coming now, instead of say five minutes ago, when two little girls could have drowned."

With the grace and dignity she'd wanted for herself, Wes hoisted himself out of the pool beside her, surging to his feet in one easy, strong motion that made her want to grind her teeth.

Only a moment ago she'd had a flashing thought that all those lean muscles of his were a bit sexy. They weren't sexy, they were maddening as hell.

"Your skirt..." he said a little oddly.

Looking down at the material which had plastered itself to her body, rendering her porno material, she tugged at it again. "I hope you're all of age," she said to the employees still standing there, and they laughed a little nervously.

She sighed. "Okay, we're fine now, so you can all go back to work. Assuming one of you stays out here to watch the pool." She glanced at Wes, unable to get past the fact she'd done an extremely childish and reactionary thing by pulling him into the water.

He hadn't yelled at her. He'd even helped her out of the water when she could have very well swum to the shallow end and gotten out herself.

Why had he done that?

She looked him over. He was every bit as drenched as she, and probably just as cold. His glasses had drops of water on them, making her wonder if he could even see her clearly.

Even more unsettling, for all his talk of wanting this job for himself, he'd been, if not exactly kind, at least honest. "Thank you."

He looked confused again and a little wary. "For what?"

"Sticking with me. For working with me, even though I know you must resent the hell out of it."

He pulled off his glasses and shrugged those amazing shoulders, so perfectly delineated in his wet shirt. "I just want the hotel to be a success," he finally said. Shoving his fingers through his hair, he sent more water flying. And then seemed to realize she was hanging on his every word. "I'd like to hear you want the same thing."

"As opposed to taking this job for the glory?" She gestured to herself, a soggy wreck. "Because from where I'm sitting, Wes, there isn't much glory."

When he just looked at her, she relented. "I want the hotel to be a success. Of course I do. I'd just like to be a part of that success. Even have something to do with it."

"As much as any of us are, you will be."

She almost felt that odd lump of emotion return to her throat, because for a minute there, wet and chilled, he *did* seem kind.

"You have mascara running down your face," he said. "It's everywhere."

Okay, not so kind. But definitely honest.

WES SPENT the day dealing with paperwork, phone calls and a handful of other things while doing his damnedest to avoid Kenna.

A few days ago that avoidance would have been directly tied into his aggravation at having to share his damn job, the one he'd wanted all for himself.

Now, he had to admit that it wasn't all about the job. He needed some space to get over the pool incident, where he'd learned a couple of things. One, Kenna had a body full of lush curves meant to bring a grown man to his knees.

He was a grown man.

And his knees were willing to take his weight.

And yet it was the second thing he'd learned that really stuck with him. For all her tough-girl, bring-it-on attitude, Kenna had a softer side, and he had to say, for just a moment there, when he'd had her in his arms, helping her out of the pool, it'd brought out the Tarzan in him.

Luckily he'd come to his senses and regrouped.

He planned on regrouping for a while longer, and was happily at it when Mr. Mallory called him.

"I hear the union meeting went well the other day. What's up for this week?"

Wes flipped open the calendar his assistant had left for him and talked business for a while before the question that he had hoped to avoid like the plague came.

"How's she doing?"

No one had to tell Wes which *she*. "She's...doing."

"Good. I had no doubt that once I convinced her to give up her wild ways, she could be a good Mallory."

For the first time Wes wondered at the pressures of being a "good" Mallory, and how that pressure would feel on the shoulders of someone like Kenna, who was clearly her own woman, with her own thoughts and ways.

As opposed to his own family, who had no expectations for him other than to be happy. And to have enough to eat.

"No problems, then?" Mr. Mallory asked.

Short of Kenna burning the place down, Wes had no intentions of being the man to complain to his boss about his daughter. "Did you expect problems?"

The older man sighed. "Look, I'll be honest. I wanted to give Kenna this chance, I *needed* to give her this chance. But...well, I know what I'm asking of you. Don't get me wrong, I believe in her, but I know she has some odd ideas, and can be a bit...shall we say strong-willed?"

Wes thought of Kenna and her concerns about the locals not getting good rates, being bothered that the restaurants didn't have specials, irritated as hell over the employee contract negotiations... Then he thought about her dripping wet, hair in her face, makeup in her eyes, sheer, lacy clothes shrink-wrapped to every inch of her incredible body.

No, Wes doubted Mallory knew what he was asking. "Everything is fine."

"Well...that's good. Carry on, then, Roth."

Carry on.

Sure. No problem. No problem at all.

Two DAYS LATER, Wes still hadn't had to deal with Kenna other than on occasional business issues. They'd divided things up and only ran into each other at meetings, where she seemed to be managing just fine.

As for himself, he was swamped. Between the ongoing renovation issues, keeping everything under control while having guests in the hotel at the same time, the accounting quarterlies and the myriad other problems associated with running a new hotel, he felt challenged enough.

When his brother Josh stormed into his office, Wes took one look at his expression and groaned. "Don't tell me I have computer problems."

"It's not the system." Josh, their computer wizard, was affectionately known as the resident "computer geek." He was tall and lean like a runner, and tended to walk with his shoulders slumped as if he carried the weight of the world. He plopped in a chair and sprawled out his long arms and legs. "It's not your computer, it's your employees. One in particular."

There was only one employee "in particular" who bothered Josh, and that was Wes's junior manager in charge of conference booking. Truthfully, it wasn't Serena's job that got to Josh, but the woman herself.

Not that Josh would ever admit it, but he had a thing for her.

As for Serena...embarrassingly enough, she had a

thing for Wes, which he'd been doing his damnedest to ignore. "What did she do now?"

"She's insane."

"Not insane, just...spoiled."

"Yeah. A spoiled *brat*."

Which apparently ran in the Mallory women. "What did she do?"

Josh didn't answer, which in itself was the answer.

"Don't tell me you asked her out again."

"Okay. I won't tell you."

"Josh, let it go. She's not your type."

"Hey, one of these days she's going to realize what a catch I am."

Josh was the baby of the Roth family, which meant that for years, ever since Wes at age twelve had first found work washing cars to help his parents pay the rent, he'd felt responsible for his little brother. It was why he'd paid for Josh's college, why Wes had encouraged him to come work here...but as a result of Wes paving the way for him, Josh didn't tolerate things well. Things being...well, Serena not giving him the time of day. "Concentrate on work. You have enough of it."

"Is that what you do when a woman is driving you crazy?" Josh asked. "Concentrate on work?"

"Yes."

Unfortunately, at the moment, like Josh, it was the woman at work driving him crazy, leaving him no respite at all.

WES THOUGHT his date that night might give him a badly needed mental break. Irene was beautiful, sexy and fun.

Or she had been when they'd met at a mutual friend's party a few weeks back. But at dinner she worried about a report she'd done earlier. She kept checking her cell phone to see if it was fully charged so she wouldn't miss any important calls. She wondered if they could stop by her office to check on something.

When they'd met, her dedication to work had been a turn-on, but tonight Wes suddenly wished she could just...be. When they were heading toward his car after leaving the restaurant—with Irene checking through her digital organizer—she stopped walking but kept working through her schedule. "My place?"

"Irene."

"Yours?" She frowned and kept her gaze glued to the small screen in her hands. "I don't think I have time to get across town and—"

"*Irene.*"

Something in his voice finally alerted her and she

looked at him. "Oh," she said slowly. "You don't want to..."

"I'm sorry," he said, while wondering if he'd lost his mind.

He watched her walk away after they'd said their goodbyes, and pictured a different woman entirely, one with long, curly blond hair, moss-green eyes and a brilliant, shimmering smile which hid things he wondered about.

With a sigh he went home to his bed. Alone. Where he decided to spend the rest of the weekend hang-gliding, surfing, whatever it took to take his mind off one unconventional, whimsical Kenna Mallory.

WHILE WES was trying not to think about her, Kenna was trying not to think about him. On Saturday night, she and Ray met for Japanese food, and over sushi discussed her life.

"Tell me everything." Ray used his chopsticks to load his plate from their shared platter. "Everything."

"Like what?"

"Like..." He waved his chopsticks in the air. "I don't know. The important stuff."

"Well..." Kenna sipped her sake. "This week we're working on quarterlies, and—"

"The juicy stuff, darling. Come on, cough up details. What are the men wearing?"

Kenna laughed. Ray shared her theory about color and attitude. "Black. Lots of black."

"Oh."

Ray looked so disappointed, she added, "But when I pointed out the lack of color, Wes wore a red tie one day and a light blue the next."

"Really." Ray's eyes went sharp. "How's it going with good old Mr. Weston Roth?"

Kenna shrugged.

"Oh, come on, you can do better than that. What does he look like?"

"How is that important?"

"Baby, baby." He tsked. "A man's appearance tells a lot about him. Come on now, does he dress slickly or as if he never looks in a mirror? Does he stand up tall or slouch over? Does he yell at everyone when he's frustrated or remain calm? *These* are the things that tell you about the guy. So spill."

"All right." Kenna set her drink down and thought about Wes, which she hadn't wanted to do that evening because thinking about him had begun to cause so many conflicted emotions within her she was feeling a little unnerved.

And Kenna hated to be unnerved. "He dresses well, I suppose. If you like conservative."

Ray shrugged.

"He definitely stands up tall and stays calm no matter what's happening around him."

"Ooh." Ray lifted a brow. "Sounds like a good match for you."

"Stop it."

"Is he mouth-watering?"

"I'm not kidding. You're taking away my appetite."

Ray laughed. "He's mouth-watering."

Kenna rolled her eyes. "We're changing the subject now—" Her cell phone rang. She looked at the caller ID and rolled her eyes again. "Why did I sign up for cell service again?"

"Who is it?"

"My father. My mother called yesterday. Clearly they've added me to their schedule, and are checking in with me in a way they haven't since I lived with them." She clicked the phone on. "Hello."

"Kenna. How's work?"

Right to the point. Wasn't that just like him. "Great. I'm great, too, by the way."

"Terrific. You know next weekend I'm throwing my annual charity benefit. Everyone will be there. I just wanted to make sure you knew about it."

Next weekend she'd planned to lie on the beach and read the financials for Mallory Enterprises from the last few years. *Much* more fun than a fancy event. "I can't—"

"Not a word I want to hear, Kenna. See you then." He hung up.

She stared down at the phone, then tossed it into her purse with an oath.

Ray grinned. "Good old dad. How close are you to getting back in the will?"

"I am not working at the hotel to get back into the will, you deranged man."

"Why *are* you doing it?"

Yes, Kenna, why are you doing it? "Because it's challenging. And because..."

"Because...?"

"Because I'm good at it."

"Well, that's a disappointing answer."

She frowned. "Why?"

"Because, baby cakes, you should be doing it for the joy of it, for the pride, because you're crazy about it and can't imagine doing anything else." He poured them both some more sake.

"That's why college was so much fun for you," he said after a quick sip. "And that's why you've enjoyed every job you ever had, because you were crazy about it, at least at the time." He smiled at her. "It's what makes you you, don't you know that?"

"I can be me without loving my job."

"You can't be the best you that you can be."

Kenna laughed. "You sound like a commercial for the armed forces."

"I'm serious." He pointed at her with his chopsticks. "A career requires passion. You, Kenna, *you* require passion."

She stared at him. "What?"

"It's true," he said gently.

"I'm missing my passion?"

"Yes."

Oh my God, he was right. He was so right. Somehow, somewhere along the way, she'd really lost it. "How do I get it back?"

"Well, as I see it, you can do one of two things."

"What?"

"Not what. Whom." A slow grin split his face. "You can do Wes."

"Ray!"

He laughed. "Kidding. But you do have to do something. Sorry, but you just have to figure it out on your own."

"Gee, thanks."

He grinned and toasted her with his sake. "You're ever so welcome."

10

MONDAY MORNING came along with a series of meetings. Kenna hit the first one armed with coffee and the realization that Ray had been right.

While this job excited her somewhat, and also challenged her, something *was* missing.

She gulped down some serious caffeine and tried to tell herself she was wildly passionate right this very minute. That today would be the day she left her mark on this corporation.

She sat at the conference table as everyone filed in for the last of the ongoing renovation discussions, and told herself that she was so passionate about this that any minute now she was going to get up and high-five everyone.

"Everything is going smoothly," Wes said as he sat. "We have only two floors not currently ready for guests, and that's short-term."

He wore a dark-gray suit today, big surprise. He looked at her through his glasses as he shrugged out of his jacket—

Exposing bright-yellow suspenders.

She grinned wide, and suddenly felt...a sparkle of passion.

"The decorators and Mr. Mallory have finally agreed on all the issues, and work commences today on both floors, which, as you know, are suites."

Suites. Kenna knew what was missing from this hotel! "Do we have any themed suites?"

Everyone looked at her, and she smiled. "You know, like a sports theme or a movie theme or... a food suite. You could attract families, reunions... And think what a honeymoon suite would do for honeymooners." She was so excited. "We could do a virgin decor, or a—" she grinned "—not-so-virgin decor."

"I'm not sure that would fly," Wes said.

Kenna looked around and saw a bunch of horrified faces.

"Our clientele—"

"Is not into virgin decor." She sighed. "Right. I knew that." Kenna set her pencil down and sat back.

And to think, she'd been bound and determined to make her mark today, one way or another. Or at least to take a solid step forward without running smack into the hard-headed, conservative wall of her father's will.

Not going to happen, and her passion went from sizzle to fizzle.

THAT EVENING, Wes stopped by Kenna's office on his way out. She watched him as he dropped a file on her desk. "What's that?"

"Projected expenses for next quarter. I thought you'd like to look."

Only more than taking her next breath. But she was tired of banging her head on the ten-foot-high brick Mallory wall. She tapped on the file. "Why should I?"

"What do you mean why?"

"What if something comes to me as I'm reading it? It seems to me that this place is a bit closed off to new ideas."

"I'm not."

"Please." She barely resisted the urge to roll her eyes.

"I'm not," he insisted, then let out a long breath. "Okay, I resisted the thought of you working here. I admitted that to you on day one."

"Because you wanted this job for yourself."

"Damn right I did. But we're sharing and I'm fine with that."

"For now."

"For now. Look, you're doing your job, you're not slacking, and I appreciate anyone who works as hard as you do," he said.

"Really?"

"Yes." He started to back out of her office. "And for what it's worth, I liked your themed suite idea."

"Until I came to the honeymoon suite, you mean."

His eyes lit with humor. "I just didn't think the board would approve of handcuffs and vibrating beds."

She lifted a brow. "I never said a word about handcuffs or vibrating beds."

Now his lips curved. "But you were thinking them."

"And, apparently, so were you." For some reason, this made her grin, too. "Uptight, regimented, controlled Mr. Weston Roth, sitting in a meeting thinking naughty little thoughts about handcuffs and vibrating beds. You're a very interesting man, Wes."

"It's shocking, the depths to me, isn't it?"

Standing, she moved around her desk so they were face to face. "Shocking."

"And by the way...I'm not uptight." Suddenly his voice didn't sound board-room and even-keeled, but slightly rough and definitely silky. "The vote might still be out on the regimented and controlled part, but I'm definitely not uptight."

"Good to know." She slipped a finger beneath his suspenders and snapped them lightly against his chest, which she could feel was hard and smooth. "You wore yellow. I'm impressed."

"My contribution to the splash of color for the day." He ran a finger over her shoulder and the bright-red suit jacket she wore.

Just that morning, standing in her hotel room in front of a mirror, she'd wondered about her need to wear something so bright, her need to stand out. What did it say about her that she expected everyone else to conform and go with what she wanted, and yet she'd never considered conforming to them in any way? "I appreciate it."

"I know."

The air suddenly seemed to crackle, and unsure about that, she stepped back.

Right into her desk.

So did he. Right out of the office. "'Night," he said.

"'Night." She didn't take a breath until he was gone.

LATER IN THE WEEK, Wes needed the files he'd given Kenna and, once again heading toward her office, he wondered what color she was wearing today.

He was really losing it.

"Can I help you?"

Serena. Man-hunting, man-hungry, man-trapping Serena. "No. I'm just looking for—"

"Me?" She smiled slow and inviting. "Well, I'm right here, silly. Right under your nose."

"Actually, I'm looking for Kenna."

"Oh," she sighed. "I just saw her heading toward the elevators. I think she was going to grab lunch."

For whatever reason, he went after her. He had no idea why, it wasn't like she was going to have his files on her.

When he got out to the parking lot in the midday heat, he immediately caught sight of her.

She was kicking her car. The back left tire to be exact. The back left *flat* tire.

"It works better if you fill it instead of kicking more air out of it," he said.

Whirling, she looked at him, for one moment completely unguarded. Gone was the sassy, confident woman who could drive him crazy with one flash of her cocky smile. Instead, he saw things in the depths of her eyes that took him aback. Things like despair and frustration and a vulnerability he'd never imagined he'd see in this woman who seemed to have everything. "What is it?" He expected her to tell him someone had just kicked her puppy or she owed half a million in back taxes. "What's the matter?"

"Nothing." Right in front of his eyes she gathered herself, managing to cloak all emotion from him in the blink of an eye. The sweet vulnerability was gone.

"Do you need some help?" he asked.

"I can handle this."

"So you know how to change a tire?"

"No. But dealing with you takes up too much energy, and I'm fresh out."

"What does that mean?"

"It means I don't feel like being *on*, Wes. Please. Just go."

She didn't want to be *on*? Is that what she'd been doing with him all this time? Was he just now seeing the real deal? "Kenna—"

"Look, I'm exactly what you think I am, okay? Just a spoiled brat mooching off her father. So just go away and leave me to my spoiledness."

"Ah, a pity party. Yeah," he said when she jerked her head up and glared at him. "That's what you're doing, you're having a good old pity party."

"Yes, well, some of us are rendered pathetic by flat tires. The some of us who haven't paid their AAA dues."

PLAY THE
Lucky Key Game

and you can get

FREE BOOKS
and a # FREE GIFT!

Do You Have the LUCKY KEY?

Scratch the gold areas with a coin. Then check below to see the books and gift you can get!

YES!
I have scratched off the gold areas. Please send me the **2 FREE BOOKS** and **GIFT** for which I qualify. I understand I am under no obligation to purchase any books, as explained on the back of this card.

331 HDL DVAQ   **131 HDL DVA6**

FIRST NAME	LAST NAME

ADDRESS

APT.#   CITY

STATE/PROV.   ZIP/POSTAL CODE

 2 free books plus a free gift   1 free book

2 free books   Try Again!

Visit us online at www.eHarlequin.com

"I know how to change a tire."

"And that might help...if I had a spare."

He sighed. Why the hell had he come out here? "I could drive you somewhere."

"No."

He nodded slowly, then turned away. If she was determined to handle this alone, then fine. Better than fine. He'd just—

"All right," she said, accompanied by a loud sigh.

He turned back to her. "All right what?"

"All right, if you're really determined to be a hero..." She lifted a shoulder. "I guess I could use a ride."

No, said his brain. *God, no. Run like hell and don't look back.*

"*Yes*," said another part of him entirely. "Where to?"

"I'll give you directions as we go."

HE OPENED the door to his car for her. She'd often admired the forest-green vintage Jag that parked beside her. "Nice."

"You'll notice it isn't black."

She was not going to laugh with him, not today. "This won't take long."

"No problem, as long as we take an extra few minutes to grab lunch."

That was all she'd meant to do. Get some fast food, anything as long as it was good and fattening with lots of French fries on the side.

And also to make a quick side trip to pay back Sarah at the Teen Zone. She'd meant to do that over the weekend, yet for some reason she'd put it off. But she didn't want to put it off anymore, she wanted to pay off all her debts, every single one.

She glanced over at Wes, who was looking a little sorry that he'd agreed to this. "I won't bite."

"Wasn't you I was worried about," he muttered under his breath, and pulled out of the lot. He hit the gas and the car responded like the honey it was. "Where to?"

"A beach in the Bahamas sounds good." She spoke lightly while her mind raced, trying to remember the way to the Teen Zone. It had been a while since she'd run out of gas in front of Sarah's place.

"Is that what you do to relax? Hang on a beach somewhere getting sun cancer?"

The last time she'd actually had the time to lie around had been in her childhood, but she had fond memories of frying herself in the sun, all in the name of a tan. "Oh yeah," she said, tongue in cheek. "I lie around on the beach all the time. Dare I ask? What would *your* ideal trip be?"

"Something a little more adventurous then sun-bathing." He downshifted for a red light. Bikinied women and buff men crossed the street, heading to-ward the beach.

Kenna leaned back and looked out the window at the flawless southern California day. "You're prob-ably one of those." She pointed to the crowd. "You're the guy that buzzes the bathing queens, flinging sand during a vicious volleyball game, or maybe just blocks their view with your surfing tech-niques."

He laughed. That he had an adventurous spirit called to her, not that she'd admit it. "Good thing we're not doing anything stupid," she said.

"Like?"

"Like dating."

His jaw tightened. "Yeah."

They drove in silence for a while after that, though Kenna would have paid to hear his thoughts since hers had left work long ago and were stuck on what she'd just said.

The thought of them going out.

It both made her wince and...yearn. "Um...turn right. Now left," she said, biting her lip, trying to re-member exactly... She pressed closer to the window as the rundown neighborhood came into view. "I don't know this place very well..."

"I do." His voice was grim, making her glare at him but he kept his eyes on the road. "What are you looking for?"

"There." She watched in relief as the Teen Zone came into view. "Pull over there."

Old, vacant houses. Graffiti on everything nailed down. Wes didn't look thrilled. "This isn't—"

"Right here, that house on the corner."

"Kenna—"

"Hold that thought," she said quickly, hearing in his tone that he was uncomfortable, that he wasn't going to let her out of the car, not in this neighborhood. The moment he braked, she opened the door and leaped out, but because she didn't want him to follow her, she peered back through the open window.

His hair was windblown, his expression behind his glasses edgy and uneasy.

"I'll be right back," she told him.

Surprising her, he reached out and grabbed her wrist. His fingers were long and strong, just like the rest of him, and she stared down, looking at his big, slightly callused hand on her smooth skin.

If she'd been one to worry obsessively, then she might freak out that one simple little touch could stop her in her tracks. Good thing she didn't worry obsessively. Much.

"This isn't a great neighborhood," he said.

"I'll hurry." She pulled free and started up the walk. Sarah's generosity had been on her mind, and she had a twenty-dollar bill burning a hole in her pocket. Something deep inside was desperately afraid Sarah wouldn't take the money, which would leave Kenna still in her debt.

Independence had become everything over the past years, *everything*. Already it had been greatly jeopardized when she'd accepted her father's job. She knew damn well she couldn't have gotten such a job on her own merit and experience, not yet anyway.

Then there was the man sitting in his car, looking at her as if she was something between a cross he had to bear and a morsel he'd like to nibble on.

Whether he realized it or not, she owed *him* as well. To her knowledge, despite how he felt about sharing the position and his doubts about her ability, he hadn't complained about her to her father, hadn't done anything other than accept her as is.

Sarah answered her knock and smiled her surprise. "Kenna. How lovely to see you. And to see you looking so well." Her smile blossomed as she took in Kenna's long, flowing dress, which, while maybe a tad sexy only because the material clung to her figure, was actually quite modest and definitely very unhooker-like. "I like the new look."

Courtesy of my old Nordstrom's discount, Kenna nearly quipped, still amazed that people paid full retail for such things. Instead, she held out the twenty-dollar bill. "I just wanted—"

"Come in. I hope you have time for a glass of iced tea?"

Kenna thrust out the bill once more. "This is yours."

"Of course it's not."

"But it is." She wagged the bill, because darn it, Sarah wasn't even looking at it. "Please. Take it. Use it for this place."

"What I could use, Kenna, if you want to help, is your time."

"I have this new job, and it takes most of my time—"

"I have a teenage girl in here right now," Sarah said. "She's eighteen and already selling herself."

Kenna's heart fell. "For drugs?"

"For clothes and food." Sarah's smile was gone. "She's too old for the foster system." She squeezed Kenna's hand. "The more people who try to reach her—"

Kenna thought about the girl inside, struggling to

survive and her throat burned in shame. Had she ever believed *she'd* had it tough? My God, how shallow. "I was just having a string of bad luck on the day we met, that's all, and now I'm embarrassed to tell you how well off I really am." She held out the money again. "I can't let you think I can't pay you back. I've told you I'm Kenna. Kenna *Mallory.* My father owns the Mallory Hotels. All of them." There was an ache in her chest at the thought of Sarah's disappointment, a woman giving all of herself to everyone around her, even a perfect stranger.

Never in her life had Kenna felt so selfish. She lifted her head to tell Sarah so, but Sarah was smiling at someone just behind Kenna. "Hello, there."

"Hello."

At the sound of Wes's voice, the ache from deep inside tightened into panic. Her first instinct was to turn around and...and smack him, but she refrained herself. Barely. "I thought you were going to wait in the car."

"Nope." He smiled at Sarah and held out his hand. "Weston Roth."

"I'm Sarah Anderson— Wes?"

"Sarah...wow. I didn't recognize you. Small world."

"It is in this neighborhood," Sarah said with a laugh.

Wes turned to Kenna to explain. "I grew up near here. Sarah lived a few doors down. She worked with my younger brother, helped me convince him to go to college instead of hanging on the streets with the worthless crowd he'd gotten into." He smiled at Sarah. "Back then your Teen Zone was a couple miles farther south. I didn't know you had one right here."

"It's new." Sarah looked around her, at the deteriorated street, at the rundown yard full of dried-up, trampled grass and crumbling brick. "Well, new to us anyway."

Kenna looked around her and thought...Wes. He'd grown up here. *Here...*

"You're a friend of Kenna's, then?" Sarah asked him, and Kenna tensed.

She wasn't his friend, she was the thorn in his side.

"Yes," he said, holding Kenna's gaze captive.

Nope. No way. She didn't buy it. Or she didn't want to. "We've got to go," she said. Pulling out the pocket on Sarah's jeans, she tucked in the twenty-dollar bill. "I'm sorry it's not more. Good luck." And she chased her own shadow to the car.

Wes got in behind the wheel as she was buckling up. "What was that about?"

"Just a visit." And now it was over. She'd go back

to her comfy new job, her comfy life and remember daily how very lucky she was. "Let's go."

"You gave her money."

"You're quick."

He studied her carefully. Too carefully, and she felt fragile, an inch from shattering. "Look, I repaid a debt, okay? Can we go now?"

"Are you crying?"

She swiped at a tear. "Of course not." What was wrong with her? Why did she feel so emotional? So on edge?

"Look, I know it's none of my business—"

"You're right about that."

"Kenna—"

Ruthlessly, she swiped at another tear. Her *last* tear. "Just drive, Wes. Can you do that?"

She felt him staring at her, but she didn't look over at him, and he let her get away with that. "Yeah, I can do that," he said after a long moment and, shockingly enough, he did.

Only he didn't take her back to work, as she'd expected. Instead, they drove up to...a go-kart race track?

She blinked at the two separate race tracks, each equipped with karts that were going *very* fast. "What is this? What are we doing?"

"Relaxing." He shoved his sunglasses on top of his head and gave her a look of pure trouble.

It should be illegal, that look, as it was more intoxicating than any drug. "Relaxing," she repeated, her voice still a little shaky. "Where's the beach?"

"No beach. We're doing this *my* way."

His way. Holy smokes, with a smile like that, aimed right at her, she'd probably do anything his way. "We're on lunch break."

"So we'll eat after." He sighed when she just looked at him. "How many hours did you work last week? Like, sixty? We're entitled."

They stood in line. Then he was slipping a helmet on her head, tucking her hair in, his fingers brushing against her jaw, his eyes locked on hers. "Ready?"

If that wasn't a loaded question. "You should know," she said, so close she could have kissed him. "This is a really bad idea. You and me...we mix like oil and water."

"I know."

"So what are we doing?"

"I haven't a clue." He stroked a finger over her jaw. "I can't remember."

"You said we were going to relax. Your style."

"Yeah. This will help."

"Help who, exactly?"

"Hell if I know."

11

THE FIRST TIME AROUND, Kenna sat with Wes in a two-seater kart. He took the track like a pro—meaning full speed—making her scream with far more terror than laughter.

Hands and body in full control of the kart, whipping them around the track, he glanced over. "Stop?"

"No!"

That caused a smile, and by the end of their lap time, she wanted to do it herself.

They picked out their karts and before the laps started, when they were side by side, waiting for the green flag, he looked over at her and revved his engine.

That was such a guy thing, she laughed. "I'm going to win," she called to him.

"No, you're not."

And true to his word, he beat her, the first two times in fact, but on the third, she pulled ahead of him in the last lap and won by a hair. She got out of the go-kart and marched right up to him.

He was grinning, until she stabbed a finger into his chest—a chest that didn't give an inch. "You let me win. Don't ever let me win."

"Then stop driving like a girl."

Oh, that did it. "One more." She got back into her kart, and on the fourth try beat him for real.

"I didn't let you win," he said when it was over.

"I know." Coolly, she let him move ahead of her before doing a little victory dance.

But when he looked back over his shoulder and caught her at it, he grinned.

And once again, the air sizzled around them.

They got back into his Jag. For a long moment, the air was tight with everything they'd repressed, with a longing and a need neither of them dared put into words.

"You had fun," he said quietly.

She lifted a shoulder. "It was okay."

"You had fun. I have the hearing loss from your screams to prove it."

"Yeah? So wear ear plugs next time."

"Say it, Kenna."

When he looked at her like that, all dangerous smile and intense eyes, she knew she'd tell him whatever he wanted to hear.

But this time, it was the utter truth. "I had fun."

"And?"

"And..." She drew a deep breath. "And if you'd stop looking at me like that, I might have the smallest chance of being relaxed. Very relaxed."

With a grin, he started the car.

THE DAYS PASSED and work went on. Kenna buried herself in it, happy enough. One afternoon she took herself to a conference room to work, where she could spread out her papers, where there was no phone and no interruptions.

And okay, maybe she didn't want anyone to see what she was working on.

For several hours, she was alone, and she read and worked away, until, without a knock, without any warning at all, the door opened and in came Wes.

He shut the door behind him and leaned against it, not saying a word.

Her heart leapt right into her throat, annoying her. More so when his gaze took itself on a little tour of her body. She wore a perfectly acceptable dress, with long snug sleeves and a tight bodice. It went up to her neck at least, and was even a rather sedate color of blue, but the way his eyes heated made her feel as though she was in a bathing suit.

She snapped shut the files and slid her notes beneath them.

"Whatcha doing?"

"Nothing." She winced at the lie. She should have come up with something.

"Nothing, huh?" He pushed away from the door to come toward her.

Damn it, she wasn't ready to show him. Standing, she lifted the file and her notes and held them to her. "I'm just doing...stuff."

"Really? What kind of stuff."

"I don't know, just stuff."

"I share with you. Now you share with me. Come on, share your 'stuff.'"

"Not today— Hey!"

They did a tug-of-war over the files for a moment, but Wes won. He stared down at them. "My postmortem acquisition file with my summary on the hotel and its merger potential with the sister hotel your father is looking at." Confused, he looked at Kenna. "What are you doing with this?"

"Well—"

"I'm presenting this information to the board next week."

"I know." She tossed up her hands. "Okay, listen. I didn't want to tell you until I'd finished my own report, but I thought I'd add it to yours. I'd hoped you'd let me present it with you, as a team. Let's just hope they're wearing color that day."

He shook his head as if it hurt. "What does that have to do with anything?"

"It's just that I've got this theory. The more color in their shoes or ties—since God forbid we pick a suit other than dark or darker—the better things go for me."

"That's...an interesting observation."

"It's true. Look at you and me. Once I got you to wear color, we started getting along better."

He shook his head. "That's just true enough to be scary. What do you want to add to my report?"

"Lots, actually. In looking back, the personnel expenses seem off. They seemed too high given what I know the employees are getting, both in salaries and benefits."

He was watching her very carefully, listening. Valuing what she was saying, which for some stupid reason, gave her a surge of pride. Good. If she didn't have passion for this job, then at least she could have pride. "When I took a closer look," she said. "I found that at the executive level, there were some interesting bonuses given."

"Yes, of course. For getting each phase of the renovations completed on time, bonuses were awarded."

"But those bonuses were all paid out whether the deadlines were met or not."

His forehead creased. "You're certain?"

"Very. If we knock that kind of crap off, we could give the employees some of the benefits we refused them."

"*Knock that kind of crap off*...you going to use that terminology in your report?"

She bit back a smile because she could hear his in his voice. "I'll try to control myself. Look, I just want to prove myself."

"Who the hell to?" He laughed. "Your dad owns the place."

But she didn't laugh with him, and he sobered. "Okay, you feel the need to prove yourself. But you've been doing that."

"I want to do more. I have good ideas, too, Wes. Ideas for the employees that would make things simpler regarding scheduling and overtime, and give a sense of company pride. I'm serious about this job, you know. Just as serious as you."

"Yeah."

"No, I mean it."

He scrubbed a hand over his face, then startled her by reaching out and wrapping his fingers around her arm, pulling her a little closer. "I know. And it's to my discredit that I haven't really done anything to help you, I've just let you go, thinking you'll get tired or bored and move on."

"Because that's what I've always done. Move on."

"I'm sorry, Kenna. You deserved more from me."

She had no idea that a man uttering those two little words, *I'm sorry*, could be so utterly sexy.

And empowering. "Don't be sorry. Make it up to me. I have research and cost projections—" She opened up her spreadsheets to show him. "See?"

He leaned over her shoulder, so close she could feel his warm breath on her cheek. "Where did you get all this?"

"I got some studies off the Internet for comparison. Here's a draft of where I see the presentation going..." With bated breath, she waited while he flipped through. "What do you think?"

He glanced at her, his eyes unreadable. "What do I think?"

She'd never cared what another person had thought about her, but she cared now.

Far too much. "Yeah." Suddenly they were much closer than she'd realized, and she became breathing-challenged.

"I'm not sure I should say what I'm thinking," he said softly. "As it has nothing, nothing at all, to do with work."

12

KENNA HELD her breath and stared at Wes, mesmerized by the look in his eyes, the feel of his large, warm hand on her arm. "It...doesn't?"

"No." They stood like that, only inches apart, so close she could see his eyes weren't solid blue, but had specks of dark gray dancing in them. A strand of her long hair clung to his throat, another to the light stubble on his jaw.

Hormone alert.

"I think," he said very quietly. "That I'd be better off taking this back to my office to look it all over without distraction."

Or temptation.

He didn't say that, but she liked to think he was thinking it. In any case, it wasn't quite the unequivocal yes on her proposal that she'd have liked to hear, but Weston Roth wasn't impulsive. He was a sharp, methodical thinker who couldn't be rushed.

Not even by lust. "Thank you," she said, gathering all the papers close. "But I'm not done yet. I'd rather polish it first." She moved to leave.

He put his hand on her arm. "You do realize that the report was done by me only because I've been here since the beginning, and that point of view is crucial."

"Maybe my point of view is crucial."

"Tell me when you're done and I'll read what you've got."

Knowing he meant it somehow added to the pressure to get it right, to actually have a crucial point of view. "Thanks," she said, liking it better when she'd thought him a jerk.

THE NEXT DAY was a scheduled managerial meeting. Wes showed up a few minutes early, wanting to be alone long enough to breathe without an audience, but when he entered the conference room, he wasn't alone at all.

Kenna had beat him there.

Engrossed in reading, she didn't even look up when he entered. "Hey," he said.

"Hey, yourself."

"What are you up to now?"

Her expression closed itself off, and he wanted to kick himself for sounding so antagonistic.

Not surprisingly, she said, "Nothing."

Nothing...Kenna was never up to nothing. He wondered what she was tackling and would have asked her about it, but Serena swept into the room.

"Your latest staff memo on the importance of customer service was brilliant," she informed Wes. "I thought we could discuss your strategies—"

"Strategies?" Josh came into the room behind her. "I've got strategies. Want to discuss them with me?"

Serena lifted a brow. "Not in this lifetime."

"Baby, you don't know what you're missing."

"Believe me—"

"Children," Wes chided. "Wait for recess."

With a snort, Josh turned away and poured a cup of coffee.

Serena smiled sweetly at Wes. "So...where were we? Oh, yes, your memo—" She broke off when Josh handed her a mug of coffee. She stared down at it, then blinked at him.

"Say 'Thank you, Josh'," Josh said.

"Thank you, Josh." She sounded confused.

Josh just smiled.

Kenna had buried herself back into her reading, making the occasional note, studying fiercely, and Wes wondered if he should be excited about their next confrontation...

Or worried.

She glanced up at him and moistened her lips, which caused his body to jerk to attention. Damn, but the line between work and feelings was being crossed.

And double crossed.

Worried, he decided. He should be very worried.

THE CLOCK in the huge, gleaming hotel kitchen chimed the hour. Twelve times. Midnight took a good long time to sound off, and since the place was empty, and also dark, the sound of it echoed eerily.

"Good thing I'm not Cinderella," Kenna muttered around a huge bite of chocolate cake. She stood in front of the large island, fork in hand, digging through a leftover cake with abandon.

It was what happened to frustrated, confused, over-stimulated and unfulfilled women, she supposed. Women who were frustrated at not being quite as good as they'd expected to be, women who couldn't tolerate their own learning curve, women feeling just a little pathetic because she...because she wanted her co-VP in an entirely inappropriate way.

In the name of comfort, she took another four-thousand-calorie bite of cake.

And then another.

WES WORKED LATE that night, hunched over his computer, hitting the keys hard, trying to keep his mind focused, but it kept circling back to Kenna.

When his phone rang, it startled him. Who could be calling at...He checked his watch. Midnight. "Mallory Enterprises."

"Weston Roth?"

"Yes. Who is this?"

"Ray Panziera, a friend of Kenna's. Listen, she's not in her room, I was wondering...is she there in the offices?"

"Hold on." He jogged down the hall but Kenna's office was dark. He went back to his. "She's not at her desk."

"Well, who in their right mind would be?"

Wes sighed. "Would you like to leave a message?"

"Oh, just wanted to see if she was up for a late-night drink. We do that sometimes."

Wes had no idea why that bugged him, but it did.

"It's no biggie," Ray said. "If I know Kenna, which I do, she's got the late-night munchies and is somewhere in the hotel stuffing her face. If you happen to see her, you might mention she could have called me to share, the bitch. Ciao."

Wes stared at the phone, then hung up. Kenna's friends were as crazy as she was. He tried to put the call out of his head, tried to get back into work, but it was no good. With a sigh, he walked out of the offices and into the elevator. Downstairs, he moved through the lobby and headed for a house phone. He had no idea why really, but something in him wanted to check on her, to make sure everything was okay. It really was late, and maybe she was sick—

Just as Ray had said, she didn't answer her room phone.

He'd now officially done his best to check on her. No way was he going to search this huge place, not at this hour.

Nope.

Dammit. There were two restaurants in the hotel, both closed. He could have tried the bar, but somehow he didn't think Kenna would go to the bar for a late-night snack.

He headed for the hotel kitchen.

The lights at the far end were on, and he strode around huge stacking trays that tomorrow morning would be loaded with baked goods, and came to an abrupt stop in front of the large wooden island.

Kenna stood on the other side of it, one hand holding a fork, the other steadying an entire sheet cake as she leaned over an opened magazine, engrossed in her reading. If he wasn't mistaken, her mouth was rimmed with chocolate.

When she saw him, the fork dropped with a clatter.

Not the magazine, he noticed, which she pressed to her chest.

Curious now, he stepped closer, not knowing what he expected. Maybe an article on "How to Drive Your Partner Insane."

Hell, even voodoo exercises wouldn't have surprised him. Pushing his glasses closer to his eyes, he leaned in. "You're reading..."

"Nothing." She hugged the magazine closer, which he could now see was *Cosmopolitan.* "I'm reading nothing. Why are you here?"

"Ray called looking for you."

"At the office?"

"At the office."

"Oh. He probably wanted to go out, we do that sometimes when neither of us can sleep." She loosened her arms and started to back away. "Thanks."

"Uh-huh." He blinked in disbelief. "You're reading..." He cocked his head to get a better look. "'How to Get Your Sexy Partner from the Board Room to the Bedroom'?"

13

UNDER THE GLOW of the harsh lights, Kenna's cheeks glowed. With heat, embarrassment...Wes had no idea, but he couldn't stop looking at her.

"It's just a magazine," she said. "I subscribe. It means nothing, honestly. In fact, I read all the articles. Here, look, I just finished this one—" She flipped through the magazine. "See? Right here. 'How to Get Your Yoga Instructor to Fall for You', and I don't even have a yoga instructor."

Then she backed away from the island, doing nothing to get rid of the chocolate on her mouth.

He stared at her lips and reminded himself that eating that chocolate off her mouth would be a very bad move. A very, very bad move. "We need to talk."

"I don't know, I really had my heart set on eating this cake."

"Kenna...what are we doing?"

"I don't know about you, but I'm eating. I heard

this thing calling my name all the way from my hotel room."

"*Kenna.*"

"Look...why do you care?"

"That you were eating cake? I don't. Why do I care that you stay in an office that was never meant for you? That one I'm not sure about. Or that you're trying so hard at this job, harder than half our employees, which I've got to tell you, is impossibly attractive. I haven't a clue, Kenna, not a single one."

She stared at him as if *he'd* lost his mind, not her. "My office is fine."

"Are you staying there because you think you deserve it? Because if you are, damn, Kenna..."

"You don't understand. You were born for this job."

"And you were born into it. It doesn't matter."

"Why are you being so nice?"

"I'm always nice."

"On my second day in this job, you gave me less than an hour to get up to speed with the union stuff. Was that nice?"

"It was reality. And now the reality is that you're here, and so am I, and we're dealing with it. Together."

"Together," she whispered. "What else are we

going to do together?" She stared at his mouth and made him hard.

But he took a big step back, and a bigger mental one.

"Right," she said, shuttering her eyes from him. "This is about work."

"Yeah. Goodnight, Kenna," he said quietly.

"Sweet dreams."

A rough laugh escaped him. "Trust me, there will be nothing sweet about my dreams tonight."

THE WEEK flew by for Kenna and suddenly it was Friday. Later tonight was her father's big annual charity event. All the employees were expected to make a showing, and seeing as the night always raised tens of thousands of dollars for various children's charities across the county, Kenna couldn't complain.

Needing some time to herself first, she actually took a few hours off work. She felt the need to get out, to drive, to walk through Old Town or Balboa Park, where she could wander through the science museum and lose herself. Or even just stand on the beach and breathe, if only for a few minutes before having to come back and stuff herself into a fancy dress and make nice.

She hit the coast first, loving the cool breeze, the salty air. Ocean Beach, her teen hangout, was packed. She got out and started walking through the sand, wanting to put her toes in the water, but everywhere she looked she saw youth and wealth and beauty sprawled out.

No one appeared to have a single issue, a single problem in their life, and even though she knew it was an illusion that it was all sun and games and vacation here for these people on this glorious summer day, it left her yearning to be somewhere else, where life wasn't so pretty, where it was more complicated, more...real.

She got back into her car and drove to the Teen Zone.

There were two girls in the yard talking. One held a lit cigarette. They weren't tanned and pretty and full of zest and exuberance, as she'd seen only moments ago at the beach. Instead they seemed hard and tired. They wore jeans snug in the butt, too long in the leg and so low on their hips Kenna couldn't imagine what kept them up. Each wore a handkerchief top that didn't come close to meeting the waistband of the jeans. One of them had a tattoo of a fern low on her spine, making it look as if she had a plant growing out of her butt. Kenna felt too old to understand why that would appeal. Both had pierced eyebrows, upper lips and chins.

Neither smiled.

Music poured out the windows of the house, where there were probably more surly, untrusting, tattooed, pierced, attitude-ridden teens.

And Sarah dealt with this every day.

Here was life, here was reality, and not understanding what drove her, Kenna got out of the car. Strange as it seemed, she understood these girls, not because she'd had to scrape by just to survive in her youth. Everyone knew she hadn't. No, she understood because they didn't fit in, and neither did she.

Two insolent gazes met hers as she entered the yard.

Kenna offered a smile. "Hi."

They looked at each other first before reacting. "Hey," one of them said reluctantly.

The other just looked at her.

"Is Sarah here?" Kenna asked.

"Yes, and she already knows I'm smoking," Tattoo Crack said, but she dropped the cigarette and ground her heel into it. She looked down at the thing a little guiltily before squatting down to dig a hole in the dirt. She then dropped the used cigarette into it, and carefully covered it back up.

Kenna met her gaze.

"She really does know," the girl said, straightening, shoving her hands into her back pockets.

As one who'd seriously tested the adults in her life at this age, Kenna nodded sagely. "Sure."

The girl narrowed her gaze, looking for all the world like a young child trying to be a grown woman. "You're laughing at me."

"Nope. If you want to kill yourself, go right ahead."

"Kill myself? Oh, Christ, you're not referring to those stupid commercials."

"I guess I am."

"They don't know what they're talking about. If smoking is so bad, they should make it illegal."

Kenna shook her head. "Should they make everything bad for you illegal? Because I gotta admit, I'd miss double mochas, caramel popcorn and cheesy omelets."

"*What?*"

"Caffeine and salt and cholesterol are killers, too."

"That's just stupid."

"Yeah. But I figure the only way you could possibly not believe smoking kills is if you live in a hole like the one you just buried your cigarette in."

Kenna smiled. "You know, the one Sarah knew you were smoking."

The other girl snickered.

"Whatever," said the smoker brilliantly.

"Nice comeback," Kenna said.

"Are you saying I'm dumb?"

Kenna lifted a shoulder. "Did you hear the word *dumb* come out of my mouth?"

"She only smokes to impress Ricky," the other girl said, rolling her eyes when the smoker chick sent her a bad look. "It's not like a habit or anything. She's been walking around with that pack for three months hoping he'll catch her with it."

"Hey!"

"It's true, Lyssa."

"Ricky sounds like the dumb one," Kenna said. "And anyway, who'd want to impress a guy who smokes?"

"Well, he's cute," Lyssa said slowly.

"Have you ever kissed a smoker?" Kenna shuddered. "Serious bad breath."

Sarah opened the front door. "Kenna!" As if they were old friends, she came down the walk smiling, arms held out.

"I'm not out of gas," Kenna said into Sarah's hair

as she found herself wrapped in a bear hug. "I have no idea why I'm here. I was just out driving and—"

"And you found yourself here, talking to two of my favorite trouble-makers, Lyssa and Debbie." She smiled at the teen girls, both of whom gave their version of a smile, meaning they bared their teeth.

"Kenna told us smokers kiss gross," Debbie said.

"I said they *taste* gross," Kenna corrected, embarrassed to have been caught discussing anything remotely sexual with teenagers. Sarah would probably be annoyed, as Kenna hadn't any right, but Sarah just nodded very seriously.

"Not only do they taste bad to others," she said. "Eventually you lose your own sense of taste entirely."

Lyssa looked horrified. "Really?"

"Really. I just put some snacks out in the kitchen. Help yourself girls, while you can still taste."

"Ricky is *so* out of luck," Lyssa whispered to Debbie on their way inside.

Sarah laughed and hugged Kenna again. "I've been trying to get her to stop carrying those things around for months. You just might have accomplished it in one day. Come on in."

"I can't." It was time to put on a pair of stockings and make nice for her father.

"Are you sure?"

"Yeah, I just came by to…" She lifted a shoulder and laughed at herself. "Say hi."

"Well, hi. Come back when you can stay longer. I have a bunch of other kids you can fix for me."

"I told you, I'm no role model."

"And I told you, you're wrong. Anyone can help, if they care enough. I'm pretty sure you care enough, Kenna."

"Sarah—"

"Just answer me this. Why did you come today?"

"To remember how stupid teenagers are?"

Sarah laughed. "They're wonderful, aren't they?"

Yeah. They were roughed up, screwed up and angry as hell, but they were wonderful.

And passionate.

Or maybe that's how she felt, passionate, in their presence, in a way she hadn't felt since she'd come to San Diego and Mallory Enterprises.

God, she hated it when Ray was right.

KENNA HUSTLED into the huge ballroom, cringing a little because she was late. Late, late, late for an important date.

Dinner had already begun.

As if God had a sense of irony, the only seat left

was right next to Serena, and directly across from the man who'd headlined her chocolate-cake fantasies the night before, so much so that she'd vowed off chocolate before bedtime.

At the other end of the table, her father glanced at his watch when she sat down.

Her mother looked slightly annoyed.

Serena tsked.

Wes just looked at her, with who knew what going through his head.

And Kenna fought the urge to keep running.

But she was a Mallory. Running wasn't an option. Screaming maybe, later, but for right now she smiled and sat.

"Well, doesn't someone think they're special," Serena muttered out of the side of her mouth.

Kenna ignored her and reached for her wineglass. She was going to need it.

"You did get the memo that said formal, right?" Serena eyed Kenna's dress. Short, shimmering and gold, it could have worked on a beach or a café or anywhere in her old life, but to a charity event... apparently not.

"Never mind." Serena shrugged. "It leaves more attention for me. You're going to lose, you know that, right?"

"Lose what?"

"What. The man across from you, that's what."

Kenna looked at Wes, who looked incredible in his tux. "This isn't a competition."

Serena laughed, her light, frothy, fake laugh. "Oh, honey. Don't mess with the queen. Watch this." She affixed an innocent look on her face. "I'll get his attention right now, right this minute. I'm...slipping off my shoe and..."

Wes nearly jerked out of his seat.

Casually, ignoring his shock, Serena lifted her wine to her mouth and whispered behind it to Kenna. "I just put my toes on his thigh. I was going for his lap but you're in the better spot for that." She slid down another inch. "There, now I can— Oh my, *someone's* built impressively."

Wes jerked again and glared at...*Kenna.*

Horrified, Kenna stared at her cousin. "Stop it. He thinks it's me."

"Christ, men are so stupid." Serena tried to catch Wes's eyes, but he was busy staring in shock at Kenna.

Kenna busied herself with her plate of food, even though the wait staff appeared to clear the dishes. Around her, everyone headed toward the dance floor, but she grabbed her plate and held on to it to keep it from being whisked away.

"I'd like a word with you."

Wes, of course. He'd come around the table. "Um..." She looked at her plate full of delicious food.

He wrapped his fingers around her arm and started to pull.

"I'm pretty hungry, Wes."

"Now."

Kenna started shoveling garlic mashed potatoes into her mouth. Maybe the garlic would protect her. "I'm eating right now, but—"

"*Now*, Kenna."

Since he'd already turned and stalked toward the door of the ballroom, she sighed. "*Thanks a lot,*" she hissed to Serena on her way out.

Serena watched Wes leave. "Oh, shut up."

"Wait a minute." Kenna laughed. "You're mad at me because he thought the toe thing was *me?* And I thought *I* needed therapy." With that, she followed Wes out of the ballroom, intending to tell him exactly what she thought of his interrupting her dinner when it was Serena who'd done the toe thing, only to be roughly grabbed by the wrist and pulled into...a storage room?

The place was dark, made darker still when the furious Wes—at least she hoped to God it was Wes—slammed the door, pressed her back against the wall, holding her there in the complete dark with his warm, rugged, *hard* body.

"What the hell was that?" he demanded.

Definitely Wes.

"You're driving me crazy, Kenna." Hands cupped her face. "Looking at me as if you want to gobble me up, making me so hot I can't see straight. Touching me—"

"Yeah, about that touching part—"

But that was all she got out before his mouth swooped down and took hers.

14

WES WANTED to devour her, and since her mouth was soft and sweet, and...and opening for his, he was well on his way.

He paused only to rip off his glasses, then resumed the hot, wet kiss. With her tongue tangling with his, thinking became impossible, and not just because of the blood loss from his brain for parts south. It was the taste of her, the feel of her arms banded around his neck, her hands holding his head captive as if she was afraid he'd change his mind and pull away.

Fat chance. She was in his arms, practically climbing up his body, warm and pliant and receptive, this woman he refused to fall for. He pulled her closer, ran his hands down her slim spine, up her legs...and *oh man*, found the bare flesh above her thigh-high stockings. "Kenna—" He skimmed his fingers over the backs of her bare thighs, and kissed her again. Kissed her until they had to come up for air or suffocate.

Slowly, she opened her eyes. "What...what *was* that?"

He set his forehead to hers. Against his chest he could feel her heart pounding. Her nipples, hard and pebbled, bored holes into his flesh.

"You know what? Never mind," she said, lifting his head by the fistfuls of hair she gripped. "Let's just do it again." And she pulled his mouth to hers.

Yes. Again. And again... Somehow in the wild kiss—wild *kisses*—his hands became full of her soft, round breasts. The thin straps of her dress slipped down, then so did the bodice, and he bent, filling his mouth with her.

He heard a thunk. Her head hitting the wall. "Oh my..." she whispered, then her nimble fingers unzipped his pants and wrapped around the biggest erection he'd ever had. "Wes?" She teased him with her fingers, stroking, until he actually thought he might humiliate himself right then—

"It wasn't my toes," she said, and rimmed his ear with her tongue.

When her words sank in, he froze. "What?"

"I tried to tell you."

He gripped her wrist and pulled back. "Not your toes. I hauled you in here, and it wasn't you—"

"Are you saying you'd have hauled Serena in here if you'd known?"

"Christ, no. Kenna...are you sure it wasn't you, because—"

She sighed and straightened her dress. "Trust me, I'd never start something I couldn't finish."

"And...now?"

"I didn't start this."

Right. He had. He'd say he was sorry, but other than not being able to walk, he wasn't. The only thing he was sorry about was that the mood had been broken. Kenna—"

"They'd better not have cleared my plate." She turned away. "Give me a few minutes before you follow, okay?"

A few minutes. No problem.

For much longer than that Wes stood in the absolute dark, still fully aroused, unable to stop thinking about how she'd felt in his hands, his mouth. How *he'd* felt in *her* hands.

How much more he wanted.

BY THE TIME Kenna made her way back into the ballroom, she'd missed dinner *and* dessert, and she placed the blame firmly on Serena.

Or she would have, if she'd been looking for someone to blame. The truth was, she didn't regret the closet incident.

In fact, she wanted another.

Wes eventually came back into the ballroom, looking subdued and bearing a plate of strawberry cheesecake, which he handed to her.

If they'd been alone, she'd have kissed him again.

She ate every bite. By the time she was done and looked around, he was gone.

She left shortly afterward as well, heading for her room. Surprisingly enough, she slept.

The next morning, Saturday, she lay in bed and stared at her fancy ceiling.

She hadn't thought about what had brought her here in a while, that being the little matter of proving her worth to the family while remaining one hundred percent true to herself. She still wanted that, but she was afraid that there were some places she would just never fit in, that maybe there were places she just didn't *want* to fit in. The job was fine, but fine just wasn't enough anymore. People didn't think liberally here, they weren't open to trying different things, to accepting something outside the box.

And maybe she was getting tired of beating her head against the proverbial wall of their resistance.

Maybe she needed to find something for *her*, something that would stir her soul and keep her going every day, and maybe that something wasn't the hotel business.

But for now she had a whole weekend, and she needed out, needed to revitalize. After three weeks of paychecks, she could have gone anywhere, but armed with a check equal to one of those weeks, she drove to the Teen Zone.

There weren't kids in the yard this time, but two men on ladders painting the house, one of them Josh from work.

The other...she blinked in the early sunlight, sure that she was hallucinating.

Or fantasizing.

Because high on the second ladder, alongside Josh, stood Wes.

At the sound of her sandals on the concrete, the two dark, handsome heads turned to look at her.

Josh smiled his reception.

Wes did not.

Shading her eyes with her hand, Kenna tilted her head back and studied them both in jeans and T-shirts, thinking it was a shame they didn't allow such dress at work because they certainly looked mighty fine in faded, soft denim. "What are you doing?"

"Painting." Josh had a streak across one cheek and his shirt, and for a guy she knew only as the Mallory Enterprises resident computer geek, he looked to be having a fabulous time.

Kenna glanced at Wes and couldn't help but yearn and burn with memories. He had paint spattered across his T-shirt and jeans, too, but he didn't grin. He simply lifted one brow and shot her a look that had her thoughts going straight to the gutter.

Every time she thought about how he'd kissed her, touched her, *everything*, she got hot and cold at the same time. Even now, her thigh muscles tightened. Her nipples hardened.

A simple, hormonal reaction to an extraordinary-looking man, she assured herself. Normal.

"Want to give us a hand?" Josh asked.

Kenna was still looking at Wes, who was looking at her right back, the sun reflecting off his glasses so that she couldn't get a feel for what was happening behind the lenses.

Josh backed down the ladder so he could talk without yelling. "It's a good cause, you know. I once spent a lot of time in one of Sarah's Teen Zones."

"You did?"

"Between that and my brother—" He hitched a shoulder toward Wes. "I managed to stay on the straight and narrow when I wasn't headed that way by myself."

Kenna stared at him for a moment before whirling back to Wes, who was still high above her on the ladder. "Josh is your brother?"

"The one and only. Original troublemaker, reformed rebel, now computer wizard Josh Roth."

"Not *too* reformed," Josh said proudly, wiggling his eyebrows. "I can still raise trouble as needed—Oops." His cell phone was ringing. One look at the caller ID had him going very still. "Well, look at that. She finally realized she wants me."

Kenna blinked. "Who?

"The fickle Mallory."

"We're all fickle."

"I'm talking the master of fickle."

"Serena." Surprised, Kenna watched as Josh answered the phone.

"This is my day off, princess, so unless you finally have the word *yes* on your tongue—" Josh went quiet, listening, then laughed. "I'm not falling for that little sniffle, so go call some other fool to come fix your home computer. I only work on Saturday for women who at least pretend to like me." Clicking off, he put the phone back on his belt and strode toward the house.

"Where are you going?" Wes called after him.

"I need sustenance."

"She's messing with him," Kenna said.

"Better him than me," Wes muttered.

"Wes—"

"He's a big boy, he can handle it."

Yes, she was sure Josh could handle it. In fact, they'd actually be good together, if Serena would ever admit such a thing.

"Why don't you grab a brush and start on the trim?" Wes asked.

"I didn't plan on..."

"What, you don't want to get your manicure all messed up?"

"What?" She stared up at him. "What did you just say to me?"

"You don't want to get your—"

"I heard you."

"Then why did you say *what?*"

"For your information, I've never painted before."

Wes smiled. "Big surprise, Ms. Mallory."

"Okay, Mr. Know-It-All."

"I am not Mr....Know-It-All."

"You are. You took one look at me on my first day and thought you knew me. You think you know everything. Now, I'll give it to you that most of the time you actually do know everything, but not all the time, Wes. Not when it comes to me. I'm not the spoiled woman you think I am. I'm my own woman, with my own ideas, but I'm not a joke."

He stared at her, then backed down the ladder and sat on the porch step. He scrubbed a hand over his face, and she refrained from telling him he now had a green streak of paint across his nose.

"You're right," he finally said.

"You should know, those are my favorite words." She grabbed a paintbrush and started on the trim. "But that's okay, as I'm a fairly big know-it-all myself."

He just stared at her.

She smiled as she started painting. "By the way, this'll be your fault if I do it all wrong."

JOSH CAME BACK out and they finished the trim, then started on the siding. Later Sarah came out with a tray of cool drinks. "I'm finished with the counseling sessions for the day," she said cheerfully. "I can't tell you how much I appreciate all this help."

Wes grabbed a soda. Painting in the sun had made him thirsty.

No, correct that. Staring at Kenna painting in the sun had made him thirsty.

And hot as hell. It wasn't that she knew what she was doing and was art in motion to watch.

It was that she *didn't* know what she was doing and was a disaster in motion to watch.

She'd looked so adorable in her fierce concentration, with her lip between her teeth, her eyes narrowed, paint splattered all across the front of her short dark-blue denim skirt and bright-red tank top and matching sandals.

He figured out about thirty minutes in, why he couldn't take his eyes off her. It was because she painted as she appeared to do everything else in life. No matter if she knew what she was doing or not, she jumped in with both feet, with no hesitation...with all her heart.

"Lyssa and Debbie asked when you're coming back," Sarah said to Kenna. "They liked talking to you."

She'd been here, talking to the kids?

"Right," she said with a laugh. "They said that, that they'd liked talking to me about smoking and smart choices."

"Well, not in those words," Sarah acknowledged. "They said they thought you were 'tight.'" She lifted a shoulder. "I just translated for you." Sarah patted her hand. "They liked you, said you didn't preach."

Kenna laughed. "I don't have much to preach about."

"You'd make a great role model," Wes said. When both women looked at him, he opened his mouth to say more, but Josh, who'd turned on the water to wash his hands, squirted Sarah.

A very wet Sarah laughed. "Oh, you're going to

pay," she promised Josh, and reached into her cup of soda for the ice cubes. *"Big."*

Josh ran into the house, followed by Sarah, and Wes laughed.

"What's so funny?" Kenna asked him.

"My brother's about to get his ass kicked."

"So are you." She brought her hand out from behind her back and used the paint brush she'd held to make a large diagonal line across the front of his white T-shirt. He was actually shocked enough to stand there, and she made another line, intersecting the first one so that he was marked with a large X.

Then she wisely whirled and ran. He went after her, but she swooped down for the hose and held it like a weapon.

"Don't even think about it," he warned.

"Oh, I'm thinking. I'm always thinking." She lifted the hose and squirted him.

The first thing he did was gasp for breath, as the water was icy. Then he took off his glasses and swiped at his eyes. Water dripped off his nose while he tried to blink the blurry, feisty, laughing woman into view.

She squirted him again, in the chest this time, making him gasp again as the cold water ran down to more vital areas.

Turning his head to the side to avoid the water in

his eyes, he stepped forward into the spray and got lucky enough to grab the hose. "Kenna? You're going to want to run from me now."

With a squeal, she did.

Despite the fact he had to put his glasses back on to aim better, he was still much quicker than she. He decided squirting her was too easy so he tackled her down to the grass, making sure she got as wet as she'd made him.

The hard part came as his senses kicked in. He was sprawled over the top of her, both of them as wet as can be, their limbs entangled, their breath comingling...

Stunned to his very core at the sudden surge of affection and yearning that bubbled up, he stared down into her face.

Her smile slowly faded, too. Her fingers lifted, sank into his hair.

He tossed the hose aside and cradled her jaw, a thumb stroking her full bottom lip. He couldn't take his eyes off her mouth. "You remember what happens when we're this close."

Her chest rose and fell more quickly now and she arched into him. "Yeah." Her eyes were glossy with excitement, and also bafflement. "Wes. What are we doing?"

"Hell if I know."

She went still, her eyes on his. "I can't do this if we don't know."

Right. She couldn't do this if he didn't know. But he couldn't if he did. Drawing a deep breath, he slowly moved to his feet, offered her a hand. "You're a mess."

Kenna searched his face, then slowly added a smile. "You're a bigger one."

Wasn't that the truth.

15

AFTER THAT, Kenna spent whatever spare time she had at the Teen Zone. It wasn't much because she worked hard at the hotel, harder than she could have ever imagined. But at Sarah's, she could *de-stress*. She felt useful and she enjoyed the company. As for the kids...well, being with them did something for her, too, something deep inside. In a way she'd never imagined possible, she liked herself when she was there. She forgot her problems, and instead concentrated on others.

In fact, she felt far more...satisfied being there than she did at her *paying* job, which she knew she'd have to think about.

But with a good five months left on her verbal contract with her father, there wasn't much she could do for now. She'd made a promise and didn't plan to renege on it.

The days flew by, and before she knew it, the next board meeting was nearly upon them. It was to be held at the Los Angeles property, and all the management of all the hotels were required to attend. It was an overnight affair, but what had Kenna sweating was the actual meeting.

Wes had finished his report on the status of the new hotel. It was sharp, to the point and brilliant—she knew because he'd given her a copy. He'd also asked about her report, twice, but though they'd talked about it and what she was working on, she hadn't yet showed him, because she hadn't finished. In a move completely unlike her, she'd drafted three different versions and thrown each away.

But playing time was over. For days she'd been working, refusing to allow herself to delete a thing. She'd added up everything she'd considered wrong with the acquisition—the bonuses, for example—and then come up with what she considered better uses of that money, such as on-site daycare, referral services for various counseling needs and additional benefits such as employee discounts at sister hotels in other cities. She researched those costs and other choices as well.

On the morning before they all left for Los Angeles, Serena poked her head into Kenna's office, looked around at the small, cramped space and shuddered. "You really do need a designer."

"Hey, you're the one who gave me this space."

"It was a joke, dear cousin. You were supposed to

get all pissy and demand a bigger place, and generally be a pain in your father's ass so he'd think you weren't worth the time he'd given you."

"Ah." Kenna couldn't quite help her smile. "Bummer that I didn't fall in line then, isn't it?"

"Yes, so would you start paying attention while I'm manipulating you? Are you ready to go to L.A. or what?"

Kenna carefully gathered her papers and stapled them together. She was officially finished. "Yes."

"You should know, tonight is the night I plan to try to coax Wes into bed. I requested a suite with a hot tub. Ever had sex in a hot tub?"

As Kenna didn't care who Wes slept with, she firmly contributed her sudden stomachache to hunger. "Nope."

"It's an amazing experience."

Okay, she cared. Slapping down her stapler, she looked up into Serena's smug face. "And I want to hear this because?"

"Because you're *not* getting sex in a hot tub tonight."

"What about Josh?"

Serena's smile vanished. "What about him?"

"I think there's something between you two."

"Bite your tongue. He's a computer nerd."

"He's smart and funny. You'd be good for each

other. You'd soften his rough edges and he'd—"
He'd soften yours. "He'd love you just as you've always wanted to be loved."

"You've been drinking, right? A little Bloody Mary with breakfast?"

"I mean it."

Serena took a step backward. "You have no idea what you're talking about."

"I've seen you, Serena, when you didn't realize...and you know what? You watch him. He watches you, too."

Looking shell-shocked, Serena sank to a chair. "He wouldn't give me the time of day."

"Are you on crack? The guy has a serious crush, Serena."

"But...I've not been particularly kind."

"Well, start."

"But I like my not-particularly-kind self." Serena stood. "Besides, we're not suited at all, of course we're not. Wes is the man for me."

She was gone before Kenna could say a word, not that she'd say the only words that might have stopped her cousin.

The words that said maybe, just maybe, Wes was the man for Kenna.

KENNA ENTERED the fabulous Los Angeles Mallory two hours later, at eleven o'clock. The place was a palace of glass and exotic plants, with amazing lighting, and again, the trademark antiques everywhere.

But Kenna didn't see any of that as she checked in. Because her report was burning a hole in her bag, and because the meeting wasn't until four, she asked which room Wes was in. Then she dropped her things off in her room—all except her report— and immediately went back out again. It was time to talk to him.

In front of Wes's door, she drew in a deep breath, glanced at her watch and knocked.

"Hang on," he said through his door. After a minute it opened a crack. No glasses in sight, he peered out, squinting. "Kenna?"

He wore only a towel, which was a bit of a shock. His hair and body were damp. A drop of water ran down his throat to his chest. Another drop slid over his ribs to the flattest belly she'd ever seen, dipping into his belly button before continuing its trail lower, disappearing into the towel to regions hidden.

At the thought of those regions, her knees actually knocked together.

And she forgot all about her report. Forgot why she stood there, tongue hanging out.

Stay on track. His body—perfect as it was—was not the issue. But suddenly she forgot the issue altogether.

Luckily he hadn't forgotten anything. He looked at the papers in her hand. "What's that?"

She forced her eyes upward, past his body and into his eyes. "Um..."

"Your report? You finally going to let me look at it? Well, come on in, then."

He hadn't unpacked, his bag was on the floor in the bathroom, which was still steamy from his shower. She tossed the report to the dresser. "Sorry to catch you at a bad time. Wes—"

"What?"

"Um..." she tried not to look at him and failed. "Seeing you half naked is weird."

"Weird like 'yuck put your clothes on' or weird like 'whoa, baby, I don't think I can keep my hands off you'?"

She laughed. How was it he always made her laugh? "Definitely choice B."

He looked at her, squinted, then grabbed his glasses. As he put them on, their gazes caught in the mirror over the dresser. Caught and held.

"Okay," he said. "And now here's another multiple choice question. Is this A, pure lust, or B, mingled in with say...a general affection?"

She lifted her gaze from his chest. "Again, I have to go with B."

He smiled, and it made her so dizzy she backed up, looking for a seat. Her thighs hit the mattress and she sank to it.

He took another step and his legs bumped her knees.

He didn't look like an important, successful VP at the moment, he looked like a bronzed, pagan god. His chest had a patch of dark hair that looked soft. She wanted to touch. His thighs were taut and powerful. She wanted to touch them, too.

And between them, at just her eye level, behind the white towel, was an interesting bulge that made her mouth go dry.

"Just one more question." He bent over her, putting his free hand—the one not holding up his towel—against her right hip, caging her in with his broad shoulders, his beautiful, rugged face on a plane with hers.

If he straightened, she'd be just about mouth level with his—

Don't go there.

"Are you enjoying the view? Wishing you were wearing just a towel, too?"

"All of the above," she whispered. His eyes were dark and full of such heat. She knew hers were, too, and also surprise because maybe she'd been blind, but she hadn't expected to feel like this about him.

Or maybe, more honestly, she'd known it all along and just hadn't wanted to admit it.

"*I'm* sure as hell enjoying the view," he whispered. "Of you on my bed." He tossed his glasses aside. Apparently he didn't need to see for this. His hands cupped her face, tilted it up for his mouth, which she met more than halfway.

A part of her wanted to look down, to see if his towel had slipped away, but then his tongue met hers, danced in a rhythm that made her hips arch up, seeking that contact with his. She wanted this, craved it and reached for him.

He kissed her again and again, stealing what little breath she had left. His mouth was as firm as the rest of him, and when he finally lifted his head, she was halfway to orgasmic bliss, from just a kiss. Needing his hands back on her, needing him deep inside her, she squirmed, but he just looked at her.

So she bit the hard sinew of his shoulder.

"That way, then?" he murmured, and she found herself flat on her back, arms over her head, staring up into one hundred and eighty pounds of aroused muscle.

"Um...hi," she said.

"Hi. You wanted me to hurry?" He dipped his head to her breast.

"Yes, please."

"I don't like to rush." Through the silk of her blouse, he pulled her into his mouth, and when her nipple instantly hardened, he very gently nipped at it with his teeth.

The low, hoarse sound that jerked from her throat might have mortified her in its clear neediness, if she hadn't already been so far gone.

He simply continued his assault on her body and senses, only now he nuzzled his way between the buttons of her blouse, and when one gave way, he nosed aside the material to kiss the slope of her other breast, grazing that nipple as well. Then, diving beneath the lacy cup of her bra, began to suckle.

Kenna arched up, writhing beneath him, making dark, horribly needy whimpers she couldn't contain. Her blouse was open to him now, spread wide so that he could touch her at will.

"I've wanted to see this," he murmured, dipping his tongue to her navel, and the little gold ring she had there. One of his hands roamed down her belly, over her thighs to her calves, then slowly back up, beneath the material of her skirt. Her legs fell open, needing his touch on the part of her throbbing with every single heartbeat, but he merely stroked his fingers over her inner thighs until she thought she would die.

Just an inch to the right, she thought desperately, *move those fingers an inch to the right.*

He didn't.

Maybe he'd get there by accident, and she scooted, arched, urged, needing that one little stroke to explode.

His tantalizing fingers dancing closer, just a little closer...

She thrust her hips upward, on a shameless mission now—

"Kenna."

Don't talk, just...do!

"Kenna."

"*What?*"

"Open your eyes."

They flew open, locked on his dark, dark gaze.

"Watch," he whispered, and stroked her over her wet panties.

With her eyes open she could see his face. His intense expression. The sheen of his skin. The huge erection bouncing free since he'd lost his towel.

He *did* have a care in the world. A very big one.

"Now," he whispered, and slipped a finger beneath her panties, unerringly stroking the one spot designed to make her go wild.

She did. She went wild. Colors exploded behind her eyes, blinding her. She went deaf, too, but not mute, and when she sobbed out his name, he towered over her, kissing her back to earth. She was halfway back, still shuddering, still clinging to him, totally shell-shocked, when there came a knock at the door.

"Wes?"

Serena.

"Shh," Wes whispered. "Maybe she'll go away."

"Wes? Open up."

He still had his mouth on her throat, still had his fingers— *No!* Kenna leaped to her feet, staggered, nearly toppled over, then managed to gather herself.

He reached for her, regret and frustration in every line of his face. "Are you okay?"

Okay? No! She was not okay, she'd just had an earth-moving, heart-tugging, mind-blowing orgasm and she wanted another, thank you very much. But she couldn't because her *cousin* was standing on the other side of the door waiting to seduce this guy with the magic fingers into bed. "Sure. I'm fine." Still trembling, she stumbled to the bathroom and locked herself in.

Not exactly mature, but it was hard to think with

all the blood in her entire body pooled and throbbing between her legs.

"Wes?" Serena knocked again.

"Goddammit," Kenna heard him swear before she heard the sound of him whipping open the room door.

Given that she'd just realized all his clothes were in the bathroom, she sure hoped he'd found his towel. Otherwise, Serena's seduction plans were going to be a cakewalk.

16

WEARING A BLACK SUIT and looking ready to rumble, Serena pushed her way in when Wes opened the door. "Weston Roth, what the hell is wrong with you? I've done everything but tear off your clothes to get you to notice me, but apparently you're a little slow on the uptake, so let me spell it out for you— Oh." Her jaw dropped open as she took him in. "*Oh.*"

Wes winced at his state of undress and the towel he held to the front of him. He hadn't meant for her to storm her way in, he'd just wanted her to stop knocking and go away. Since he could feel a breeze on his bare butt, he backed to the dresser, and for his effort got a drawer handle in a very bad spot. "I'm busy, Serena." He'd left the door open in an invitation for her to leave.

"You're...wow." She eyed him from chest to toes, then back up again.

"Serena—" He stepped back so hard the drawer handle became his new best friend.

"Wes..." She leaned in. "Did you hear the *I want you* part of my speech?"

"Yes, Serena, he heard." This from a grim Josh, who walked into the room.

Wes's room, which had turned into Grand Central Station.

Josh took one look at Wes and let out a low laugh. "I see you have a problem." Then he turned back to Serena. He took her shoulders in his hands and hauled her up on her toes, only an inch from his mouth. "And here's mine—"

"Now, you wait just a minute—"

"Shut up, Serena." He spoke gently, still holding her. "Now, the way I see it, you have a little attention deficit disorder you never outgrew. You aren't getting any good hot sex, and it makes you trouble personified. Well, guess what? I've got a deal for you."

"Put me down."

"Nope." Josh tossed Wes a look over his shoulder. "You want to give me a minute here?"

"I would, but I have another little problem in the bathroom."

"Like?"

"Like it's currently being held hostage, along with all my clothes, by another fairly agitated woman."

Josh stared at him, then grinned. "Oh man, you always did get all the fun."

"Could we hurry this along by any chance?" Wes growled.

"Right." Josh turned back to the squirming Serena, who clearly was not used to being manhandled. "Okay, listen up, we have to put this into high gear on account of my brother and his woman dilemma. You want attention from a man? I've got plenty. You want a man who knows where he's going and what he's doing? I'm him. You want someone who will be crazy about you, and never, ever, fail you?" He set her on her feet and slipped his arms around her. "I'm that man, Serena."

She went very still. "What?"

"I think you heard me. I might not be president of the hotel, or even VP, but I have a job with lots of potential and I'm damned smart. And every bit as ambitious as you are. We're a match made in heaven, baby."

She shook her head, so bewildered she apparently forgot to keep fighting him. In fact, she fisted her hands in his shirt and hauled him closer. "Say it again."

"All of it?"

"Yes," she demanded. "Please?"

Josh's smile was dazzling. "I'm crazy about you.

Now, you say that you think we have a shot and let's get out of here. My poor brother has issues, and if I'm not mistaken, a dresser attachment disorder."

Wes fully expected Serena to bite Josh's head off. Instead she smiled demurely. *Sweetly.* "I think we could have a shot."

Josh kissed her hard and long, which might have gone on forever if Wes hadn't cleared his throat.

"Right." Josh grinned, and herded Serena out of the room.

Wes locked the door and stormed to the bathroom. "Open up, Kenna."

She cracked the door. She'd buttoned herself up again, very neatly. A shame. He'd have to undo it again. He dropped his towel and muscled his way in, tugging her out of the bathroom and to the bed.

She went with such ease, he knew it was what she wanted, so he followed her body down with his. With one wrench, he separated the material of her blouse. Buttons flew.

"Um—"

Unclasping her bra, he drew both that and the blouse off her shoulders. "There. That's a little better."

She gasped as his mouth came down on one of the breasts he'd bared, then she writhed helplessly under the erotic assault.

He slid off her skirt, then her panties, leaving her as naked as he. "Now," he said, triumphant, towering over her.

"Do you think Serena and Josh are—"

"Yep. And with any justice at all, so are we."

She stared at his mouth. "Wes—"

His mouth covered hers because he didn't want to hear why this wasn't their smartest move. He already knew, he knew every reason intimately and didn't care. He wanted to lose himself in the heat, in the need, in the moment, feeling as blindsided by her now as he had the very first day she'd marched into his life.

They kissed for long moments, and he felt the most intense hunger he'd ever experienced. Intending to satisfy that hunger, he slid down her body and kissed her from head to toe until they were both shaking.

"Now," she gasped.

Condom. He needed one. "Uh...hold that thought." He staggered into the bathroom, groping through his bag, inadvertently dumping it to the floor. Damn it. Finally, snatching up a little foil packet, he tore it open on the way back to the bed. "Where were we?"

"If you've forgotten, you have serious ADD."

He laughed. He didn't understand how he could

want her so badly his entire body shook, but the wanting filled his very being. Getting the condom on turned out to be a bit tricky, as he could hardly see straight, but he managed, then lifted her hips and finally, finally sank into her body.

Her body was hot and tight, and he felt his toes curl from just his first thrust. With all his might, he tried to make it last. He thought about the quarterlies, the money he'd lost in the stock market, *anything*, but with a high, thready sound, Kenna shattered in his arms, and that was it. He shattered, too.

For long moments afterward, he continued to quiver like a baby, and actually, it was extremely possible he'd died and gone to heaven.

But then her arms banded more tightly around him, cutting off his air, making his chest hurt.

Nope, definitely still alive.

He rolled with her so that he lay flat on his back, with her curled at his side, and braced himself for that usual after-sex smothered feeling.

It didn't come. Something else, another feeling entirely, came instead. It'd happened without his realizing it, but it *had* happened. He wanted to be with her.

He reminded himself they were too different. She was whimsical, fanciful. Happy to just...be.

He was driven, hungry and ambitious.

And full of crap.

Fact was, he'd never had a good handle on Kenna. She might be fanciful and whimsical, but she worked hard, too. And she had plenty of drive and passion.

He had the Teen Zone memories as proof of that.

So did he...had he actually, maybe fallen—

"Wes?"

"Yeah?"

"I didn't sleep with you so you'd put our reports together."

He laughed.

She didn't.

With a sigh, he looked into her face. "If I'd thought so, we wouldn't have done this."

"I just wanted to say it."

"Well...thank you."

She sat up. "I've got to go get ready."

But he wanted round two. "So...later, then?"

She looked startled. "Later what?"

"Later...more."

"Oh. Um..."

He ignored his heart shriveling, along with other parts of him as she bent for her clothes, her cute, edible little butt wiggling as she shimmied into her panties. "I'll take that as a no." He got to his feet, thinking he should have stuck to his usual routine after sex and gone to sleep.

She found her blouse, swore when she remembered the torn buttons. Tossing it down, she went into the bathroom and the bag he'd dumped on the floor, rummaging until she came up with one of his shirts. Shoving her arms in, she hauled her skirt over her hips, shimmying a little to get everything tucked in, belatedly finding her bra. That got stuffed in her pocket. "Wes..."

He looked into her eyes and saw a surprising amount of nerves. "It's okay," he said. "It's going to be okay."

"Are you sure?"

Hell, no. "Absolutely."

She headed toward the door, in *his* shirt, for the second time in an hour fully dressed to his being completely naked.

"See you at the meeting," he said. "I'll bring the reports."

She looked back at him. "You don't have to bring mine."

"Shut up, Kenna."

"I just meant that this—" She gestured to the bed. "And that—" She looked at the report she'd left on his dresser. "They're not all tied up together or anything."

"Look, I know that *this*—" He jerked his chin to the bed. "And *that*—" And then the report on the dresser. "Aren't tied up."

She nodded in relief and left.

And then he was alone, wondering how the hell was it that he'd been ditched, when he hadn't even known he wanted both *this* and *that* in the first place.

WELL, SHE'D DONE IT, hadn't she? She'd finally caved in to the attraction between her and Wes, and what had it gotten her? A perfect orgasm.

Two, in fact.

In her own room she showered and dressed, then stalked downstairs with moments to spare before the board meeting. The conference room was set up with food and drinks, but she'd lost her appetite.

What had she done? She'd mixed business and pleasure, and how. *That's* what she'd done. How in the world had this happened? She felt...so misdirected. Lost.

Alone.

Stupid.

"Kenna."

Whirling, she faced the man who only a little while before had had her whimpering and begging him to finish her off.

He was solemn now, his mouth tight, his eyes tired and tense behind his glasses.

He was holding her report. "You okay?" he asked.

She started to nod, then slowly shook her head. "I feel...a little mixed up."

"Like you were hit by a truck?"

"Yes."

"Yeah, I felt the same way. Until I thought about it." He looked at her for a long moment. "We started out pretty adversarial, didn't we?"

"Pretty much, yes."

"But it didn't stay that way," he said. "I'd like to think we've built a mutual respect, even a friendship."

"What just happened wasn't about respect or friendship."

"But it was good." He smiled, and her heart tipped on its side.

Thank God she'd finally gotten it right and worn waterproof mascara.

"It doesn't have to be so complicated, Kenna."

Right. It didn't.

He held out her report. "Let's start here, only because we have to. Are you ready for this?"

"Why? Do I have something to do in there other than be Mr. Mallory's daughter?"

"You don't like being your father's daughter?"

"Sure. Outside the boardroom."

His gaze caressed her face. "Your report is good. Go for it in there."

She looked around to make sure no one was listening. "Are you sure that's not the sex talking?" she whispered.

He looked shocked. "What? I thought you said these were two separate issues."

"Just checking. I mean, if you say the report's good, then...you get more sex later, right?"

He grinned. "Would that actually work?"

She had to laugh. "I'm not too ashamed to say yeah, it would work, but tell me it's not so anyway."

"It's not." He lost the grin and went serious. "Do it, Kenna. Go in there and do your thing. You're good at it."

"I am." She looked at the food spread. There were chocolate doughnuts. Good. She needed one. Two. This was definitely going to be a two-doughnut meeting.

17

THE ENTIRE TIME Wes spoke in front of the board, the only person he was aware of was Kenna. Everyone appeared to be listening, nodding, whatever, but he didn't really care...except about what Kenna thought.

Would she do it? Stand up and get what she wanted?

"Excellent, Roth," Mr. Mallory said when he'd finished and everyone had applauded. "Thank you. The newest addition is coming along better than I had hoped, and we know we owe that to you."

"I didn't work alone."

Mr. Mallory looked at Kenna. "Yes, my daughter. I'm thrilled she's been able to help you."

Kenna's smile didn't falter, but then again, she was a Mallory. Tough. Resilient. "She more than helped me," Wes said. "And she has a report as well."

Mr. Mallory lifted an eyebrow and looked at his daughter.

Kenna stood, and with a perfectly calm voice and steady hands, told every board member what she thought of the bonuses that had gone to executives instead of being trickled all the way down the line to the employees who needed it more, what she thought about the lack of available child care for their thousands of employees. She told them what she thought about their nonexistent programs for maternity and paternity leave, and what she believed was a far more fair package. She discussed costs and suggested alternatives.

Then her father stopped her. "Expensive ideas."

"Yes," she agreed. "But if you look at the financials, worth it. Especially considering that in the long run, some of these things are cheaper and have a bigger payoff than the executive bonuses."

Her father nodded. "I'll think about it. Thank you, Kenna. Next on the agenda?"

Her expression carefully blank, Kenna sat down.

Wes waited for her to look at him so he could smile at her, anything to make her look...happy, but she didn't.

Mr. Mallory moved the meeting along, not addressing his daughter again, not even when the meeting was over.

Wes supposed that's when he realized his loyalty had shifted.

Maybe, if he was being honest, he'd felt it shift way back on that very first day he'd met her.

KENNA DIDN'T go to Wes's room that night. She intended to soak in her tub and let herself have a good, long, rare pout.

But Wes came to her.

When she opened the door to him, when she moved aside so he could come in, they didn't talk.

They didn't even try.

What they did do was their damnedest to burn up the sheets. The shower. The floor in the bathroom.

And in the deep dark of the night, still without saying a word, she fell asleep in his arms.

And woke up alone. He'd left a note on her pillow, written on the hotel stationery.

A smiley face.

It made her laugh. The truth was, she was glad to wake alone, glad for the time, because what had happened here in Los Angeles, both with Wes and in the boardroom, had thrown her a little. She needed to separate it all in her head, needed to think.

By Monday she thought she had it all sorted out. Some of what she and Wes had experienced had been adrenaline, some genuine affection. But mostly it had been pure lust.

And now it was most likely out of their system. In light of that knowledge, work was simpler than she'd have thought. Meetings kept both her and Wes from saying anything to each other except business-related talk, and after a brief flash of disappointment, she decided that was a good thing. They didn't need to complicate anything with a discussion.

Besides, what would she say? *Thanks for the greatest sex ever? I'll never look at a hotel bathroom counter quite the same way?*

Can we get a hotel room tonight, too?

After work, she went to her parents' house. The Monday-night Mallory family dinner proved to be as torturous as any, and less than three minutes into the thing, Kenna wanted out.

Ray had tried to talk her into dinner with him and his latest significant other. She should have gone, she'd have been so much better off.

Instead, here she was. Feeling this odd restlessness she didn't know what to do with. Damn, she hated a pity party, especially her own. She bucked up. *No more pathetic thoughts, not a one.* She promised herself dessert if she managed to keep a smile on her face. A *big* dessert.

Everyone around her had someone. Her mother and father, of course. Her aunt and uncle. Then Serena and Josh arrived, gazing into each other's eyes until Kenna felt nauseous.

"Dinner is nearly ready," her mother said. She stopped to look more closely at her daughter and frowned. "Honey? You look a little peaked."

Yep, most definitely peaked.

"You're working too hard. I knew it. I told your father so."

"Which of course made him laugh." Kenna watched Serena and Josh come around the corner. Josh's tie was crooked. Serena had a goofy smile on her face.

"Laugh?" Her mother frowned. "Why on earth would he do that? Actually, he agreed with me. Told me how much effort you've been putting in."

"He did?"

"Your father isn't a sentimental man, Kenna. You know that. It isn't often he'll wax poetic over hard work and dedication, but he notices. Don't you ever think he doesn't." Her mother checked her spotless dress, smoothed back her hair. "Isn't Serena lovely tonight with her new beau?" She moved into the kitchen, and for lack of anything else to do, Kenna followed her. "I hope he treats her right."

Kenna laughed and helped herself to the tray of hors d'oeuvres on the counter. "Don't you have that backward? I hope she treats *him* right."

"Is Josh a good man, then? Oh, good. Your aunt was so worried. I know he doesn't come from much, not that that really matters, but—"

"He's a good man. His family is—"

Strong.

Smart.

Sexy.

And suddenly she wanted to see Wes so badly her body hummed.

"Kenna." Her father came into the kitchen. "We haven't had a chance to talk privately since the meeting. You did great."

"What?"

"Something wrong with your hearing? Your proposal was solid."

"You hated my proposal."

Her father looked shocked. "Of course I didn't."

"You didn't agree with a single point."

"Yes, well, that was business. But you were well-prepared, you were smart, sharp and articulate." He smiled. "I was proud of you."

"You were..." Stunned, Kenna looked at her mother, who was also beaming with pride. "Proud."

"Absolutely. Keep it up. We've got high hopes for you."

"In the hotel."

"In the business, yes."

Kenna drew a deep, shaky breath. "Dad, I've given it a shot, and I'll give you the rest of the six months I promised you, but this is not going to be a life thing for me. I just don't have the...the passion for it."

"Didn't you just hear me say how pleased I am with your progress?"

"Yes, and believe me, I've always wanted to hear it." Only the funniest thing, the world didn't stop. The heavens didn't sing.

Her heart didn't soar.

And no one was more surprised than herself when she said, "I'm so sorry. I just really want to do something else."

"What?"

She smiled, but it was a little wobbly because though it had just come to her, she thought maybe she'd known it all along. "I don't want to say until I cement the position. Which I won't do until I give you the time I promised you."

Her father looked at her mother, who nodded. He sighed. "I wanted to push you into this, I wanted it to work for you. But I'm not going to hold you to the six months, not if it's not working. I'm not that self-ish."

Kenna stared at him, then hugged him hard. "Do

you remember that Ferrari you dangled in front of me?"

"Of course. Don't tell me you still expect it."

"No. Because I have a far better use of that money. It's for a good cause."

He gave her a long look. "Legal, right?"

She laughed and hugged him again. "Very legal."

SHE MEANT to go straight to the Teen Zone to see Sarah, but she made a detour and drove by Wes's house. She'd never been there, but she'd asked her father for the address. She just wanted to talk, to tell him the things she'd been thinking about...and okay, maybe she'd decided they shouldn't suffer, they could have mindless sex. All in the name of therapy, of course, but he wasn't at his small and shockingly adorable cottage on the beach. She left him a note on his front door.

A smiley face.

Onward. She drove the streets of San Diego toward the Teen Zone because what she needed more than mindless sex, what she really wanted, was to see if her glimmering idea could be turned into her passion.

There was a kid sitting on Sarah's steps, but it wasn't until Kenna got directly beneath the light that she saw it was Lyssa. "Don't tell me you're out here lighting up," Kenna told her. "I don't need lung cancer, thanks very much."

"I'm not smoking." Her voice broke. "Just... hanging."

And crying. Damn it. Kenna sat next to her and resisted the urge to hug her. "Is some guy being a jerk?"

"They're all jerks."

"At least at your age, they are." She sighed. "Ever read *Cinderella*?"

Lyssa leaned back and gave her a hard look, reminding Kenna this girl hadn't had anything remotely related to a fairy-tale childhood. "Are you going to tell me my Prince Charming is waiting just around the corner?" she asked.

Kenna smiled. "Well...yes."

"Does he have a car?"

Kenna leaned back and studied the stars. "I couldn't say, but I know for sure he's out there. Somewhere."

"He's sure taking his sweet time about finding me."

"Yeah." Kenna had always had the same problem. Actually, she'd never really looked before. She'd never really been one of those girls who'd dreamed about marriage, two-point-four kids and a white picket fence.

All she'd ever wanted was to do her own thing, and she'd been pretty good at that so far.

So maybe, just maybe, it was time to think about Prince Charming.

But surely Prince Charming, whoever he was, wouldn't appreciate her wanting wild sex with Wes. That would be a big no-no.

Maybe she should just make *Wes* her Prince Charming.

Her heart actually went pitter-patter at that, because he was gorgeous and funny, and—

And she was already more than halfway in love with him.

Oh boy.

"Kenna?"

She realized Lyssa was looking at her. Where were they? Oh yeah, Prince Charming. "Just don't kiss too many frogs while you're waiting for him to show up. Better yet, don't sit around waiting for him, you go pick the one you want."

Lyssa laughed and swiped her eyes on her sleeve. "Just go get him, huh?"

"Yeah, but if he wants to do more than kiss you—"

"Turn him into a toad?"

"Yes. An ugly one, with warts."

Lyssa laughed again, and that felt good, hearing

her, seeing her smile, knowing she'd helped, she'd really helped.

They watched the night for a few more minutes before Lyssa said, "So where's your prince? Is he out there also?"

"According to my own rules, he has to be."

"Have you met him yet?"

"I'm hoping." She watched a star fall. "I'm hoping a lot." She gave in to temptation and hugged Lyssa, then stood up. "I've got to see Sarah."

"What about?"

She took a deep breath. "I'll tell you after it's done."

Lyssa blinked. "Okay." She waited until Kenna had reached the front door. "You going to work here?"

"Are you this smart in school?"

"What, like I couldn't figure it out?"

"All right, I want to work here." She didn't just want to make her father donate the price of a Ferrari and visit once in a while. She wanted to take the additional college courses she needed to counsel the kids. That combined with her life experiences, and she figured she'd be great.

Passionate.

The hours would be long and the pay short, but what was new about that? In the meantime, she'd volunteer. Just like this, giving her time and help in any way that she could. "Would you like if it I did work here?"

Lyssa lifted a noncommittal shoulder. "Sure."

Not exactly a resounding endorsement, but Lyssa was a teen and didn't do resounding.

But then Lyssa rolled her eyes. "Duh, Kenna." She smiled widely. "You'd be great."

Yeah. She'd be great.

18

AFTER TALKING to an excited Sarah, Kenna practically danced out to her car. She was so happy, so excited, she could hardly contain herself.

Her life was actually, genuinely, on the right track. There was a sticky note on her windshield—with a smiley face on it.

Taking it off the window, she hugged it close to her chest, feeling a ridiculous grin burst onto her face.

Mindless sex, here she came. A perfect way to top off the night.

She drove to his house and took a moment to admire the full moon.

Then she laughed at herself. There was a tall, dark and sexy man just inside, and she was standing here looking at the moon. She had to laugh at herself.

"What's so funny?" came a husky voice from the top step.

Wes.

"I was just thinking, I'm standing out here sighing over the moon, when I could be inside..." She met his gaze. "Sighing over you."

"It *is* a beautiful night. I was sitting here thinking about a long walk with you."

Her laugh was breathless. "And here I was wishing we were doing something fast and reckless and exciting."

"We?"

A loaded question, one she wasn't sure she had an answer to.

He came close and smiled, a sexy one that made her heart stutter. "That one little word *we* scare you, Kenna?"

"Only slightly more than hell, yes."

"You missed me."

"Maybe. Wes...my father released me from my contract. The job is all yours."

"What?"

"I'm going to go back to school. I'm going to work at the Teen Zone. It's what I really want to do, it's what put this smile on my face."

"And I thought that was me."

She laughed. "*You* turned the smile into a grin."

"Okay, then." He sobered, touched her face. "I thought you liked your job."

"I do. I like it. I like it a lot, actually. But I realized I don't love it, not like you do. It doesn't drive me,

Wes, and I want something that does. I want that so badly."

"You know I'll miss you at work."

"That'll pass."

He put his hands on her arms. "I doubt it," he said so seriously, she felt a lump in her throat.

"But I won't miss you *outside* of work." His eyes heated. "Or I'm hoping I won't."

"You won't," she whispered.

"Let's go."

Her heart leaped. "To do something fast and reckless and exciting?"

"I was thinking of long and slow and sweet." The blatant look of desire behind his glasses made her hormones rev. "Or at least something halfway between. Up for a compromise, Kenna?"

Were they still talking mindless sex?

Still holding her hand, he brought it to his mouth, let his lips linger as he gazed at her over their entangled fingers.

"Yes," she said, her bones liquefying. "A compromise."

HE TOOK HER INSIDE the house he'd bought with his first bonus from Mallory Enterprises seven years before. It had been a dump back then, but he'd slowly renovated the place, made it his.

Now, when he could have bought nearly any other house he wanted, he wouldn't have traded it for the world. In the years since, he'd purchased places for his parents and his brother, but he'd stuck with this one for himself. It meant something to him that he'd come from nothing. That he'd rebuilt this house from nothing.

That he'd made himself a home.

He opened the front door, watching Kenna take in the airy, open space that was his living room.

"This is great," she said. "Are we going to—"

"Make love." He pulled her to him, slipped his arms around her. "We've had sex, fast and hot and reckless. But we haven't made love, Kenna, long and slow and sweet."

She laughed a little, and backed up. "But I didn't have anything against the fast and reckless sex."

"Are you nervous because I used the love word now?"

"Don't be ridiculous. Nothing makes me nervous."

"I think *I'm* making you nervous."

"Wes..."

"We're still different, you know. Nothing's changed there."

"Not that different, I've come to realize."

"Different enough."

"Let me show you we're not, let me prove it."

She looked so excited and nervous and terrified all at the same time, poor baby.

He knew just how she felt. He pulled her close again, trailed his mouth along her jaw, loving the feel of her body against his as they swayed together in the middle of his living room. "I should tell you...I work hard and play hard. I thought women were just a part of the play. They're not. You're not."

"I know."

"You work hard and play hard, too," he said, and let that sink in.

They weren't that different.

"Come see the rest of the house with me." He showed her the kitchen, the deck...his bedroom.

She laughed at his unmade bed, then squealed when he scooped her up and tossed her onto it. Her cheeks were flushed, her eyes slumberous. Her long hair tumbled over her shoulders.

She looked so good in his bed, he planned on keeping her there a while.

A long while.

She came up to her knees in the middle of the mattress, looking right at home there. Kneeling on the bed with her, he cupped her face, kissed her jaw, her throat, nibbling at the corners of her mouth before he finally settled his lips over hers, scooping her closer, loving the feel of her warm curves against his body.

As he undressed her, he felt her pulse hammer beneath his fingertips. He intended to go slow, give as much pleasure as possible, but as he peeled off her clothes, exposing her body to his gaze, his own pulse hammered in his head.

So hot, so...his. Her body curled into him, her breasts and hips flush to his, moving, arching as the need built to unbearable heights.

Tugging his shirt free, she tossed it aside, then ran her hands over his chest and arms with a look of wonder on her face. "You're so beautiful." Then she shoved him to his back on the bed and pulled off his pants.

He'd barely taken a breath before she straddled him, wrapping her fingers around his erection, bringing him to her hot, wet—

"No," he managed to say through his clenched jaw, and rolling, tucked her beneath him. "Not yet."

Her hands, caught in his, flexed as she stared up at him. Not yet? What did he mean not yet? "Why not?"

"I told you. Long and slow and sweet. Or at least at a speed somewhere below wild and crazy. We're going to make love, Kenna. Haven't you ever made love before?"

Panic wove around her heart. "Wes—"

His tongue circled her nipple.

She nearly jerked out of her skin. "I don't think—"

"Perfect," he murmured. "Go with that." Lifting up a fraction, he blew on her wet skin. She watched him watch her intently as the tip beaded tightly under his administrations. Then he drew her into his mouth, and she writhed against him, helpless, mindless against the onslaught of emotions.

"Easy," he whispered, trailing his mouth over her quivering belly. "We have a long way to go." His tongue dipped into her navel, then lower, until she felt his warm breath on the inside of her thigh.

"Wes—"

He kissed her, *there*. "Yum," he said, and used his tongue.

She nearly shot off the bed, but he held her still beneath him, slowly, surely, purposely driving her out of her mind. Because he knew her, because she'd let him know her, he was able to torment her, for one long, humming moment holding her quivering and shuddering on the very edge.

"When...I can...breathe," she panted. "I'm going to...*so* torture you back."

He treated her to one perfect stroke of his tongue and sent her skittering into an earth-shattering climax. Surely such intensity, such unbelievable reverence and desperation had never existed before now. Her entire body shuddered and clutched, and finally, she felt his weight shift, felt him reach for a condom.

"Oh, no," she managed, and flinging her hair from her damp face, sat up. "My turn." She shoved him to his back, looking over his body, from his broad shoulders to his tough chest and flat belly...

To the part of him standing at attention. Needing attention. "Hmm. Look at that."

"Kenna—"

"Shut up, Wes." She took her time looking, then touching, then tasting...and only when the breath was sowing in and out of his lungs as if he'd run a marathon, when his body was gleaming, when he'd whispered her name over and over in a plea that made her wet all over again, did she sit back on her heels. "Yep, that should do it. We're even."

"Condom," he begged, and reached for the night stand.

She helped him, then put her lips to his damp shoulder, surprised when he cupped her face for a sweet, tender kiss. "Now," he said, and rolled her beneath him. "The slow, the tender. The gentle." As he eased into her she was blown away by the sense of homecoming, a rightness, a joy that couldn't be explained.

It was the most intimate thing she'd ever experienced. She stared at him, her anchor, her lifeline. He'd been right about one thing, this was more than that mindless sex she'd come for.

If that's what she'd really come for.

He smiled as if he knew, as if that was okay with him even, and began to move, and she nearly died.

Definitely more than sex, but she had no idea what to do with that knowledge other than close her eyes and let it take her.

19

KENNA WOKE UP to the early sun shining in her face. Squinting, she sat up and blinked.

She was naked, still in bed. But not hers.

The room was warm from the rays blaring in the window. The scent of the ocean wafted in, too, ruffling the gauzy curtains.

There were other sights. Three discarded condom packets on the nightstand. And Wes's pillow, which she'd stolen, lay in her arms. Like a silly lovestruck teen, she smashed her face into it, inhaling deeply. She couldn't wait to hold him again, couldn't wait to look into his eyes and—

Hold it.

The scent of bacon and something cinnamony came to her then, and she lifted her face in time to see a shirtless Wes slipping back into the room, holding a tray. He wasn't wearing his glasses, so he was giving her that adorable, sexy, squinty-eyed look that told her he was straining to see.

She was glad for the lack of glasses on his part, because it hit her right then, like a one-two punch.

She'd fallen all the way in love with him. Heart-pounding, pulse-drumming, howling-at-the-moon, crazy-about-him love.

Clearly mistaking her half awed, half horrified expression for lust, he grinned wickedly and set down the tray. "Hungry?"

"Um...yeah." She put a hand to her belly, knowing it wasn't hunger pangs making it quiver.

"You're going to sidetrack me from my mission," he said hoarsely, staring at her body as he put a knee on the bed.

The top button of his jeans was undone, and feeling shameless, she reached for the others. So she'd fallen in love with him. So what? He didn't have to love her back, not right now, not yet, not as long as he kept looking at her like that.

"Wait." He put a hand over hers on his jeans.

He looked suddenly so nervous that she sat back. She would have reached for the sheet to cover herself, but he'd sat on it. "About last night," he said.

Oh, no. Nothing good ever started that way. He was going to dump her. She tried to tug the sheet free, but Wes simply place a hand on either side of her hips and leaned over her. "Kenna—"

"I need my clothes." They weren't on the floor.

She couldn't be dumped while buck naked. "Wes, where are my clothes?"

"Yeah, about that, too. I've taken your clothes hostage."

"This isn't funny."

"We'll get to that. Kenna, you're amazing. I want you to know that. You're independent and smart and incredible under pressure. I love watching you work."

She stopped craning her neck for sight of her clothes and went still. "This is about...work?" She wished he'd release the sheet because she was beginning to feel very, very naked here.

He laughed and shook his head. "Okay, no. You know what? Starting over now." Reaching out, he drew a strand of her long hair through his fingers, smiling with a sort of soft tenderness that quite frankly stole her breath. "This is *not* about work. This is about what's going on between us. I want it, Kenna. I want all of it. And I want it to be permanent."

She forgot all about her missing clothes and stared up into his dark, dark eyes. "Did you just...in a very roundabout way...say you love me?"

"Yes."

Her mouth went dry. Her heart, her poor confused heart, started a heavy, erratic beat. "Do you think you could say it again with the words this time?"

"Kenna." He blew out a huff of air and hauled her up to her knees in the middle of the bed to face him. "I'm holding your clothes hostage in the same way you're holding my heart. I've imagined falling in love before, it was always a sort of long-term thing, something for down the road. *Far* down the road." He cupped her face. "But apparently, love isn't something you plan for. I certainly didn't plan this, but from the first moment I saw you—"

"Don't you say you fell instantly for me," she said, shaking her head, trying to back away. "I know I drove you crazy. There was nothing instantaneous about how you felt for me."

"Oh yes," he said with a ragged laugh. "Yes, there was. You drove me crazy, you might always drive me crazy—" He laughed again when she smacked his chest. "But God, Kenna, I've never felt like this for anyone, have never loved another so very much."

It was hard to talk with her heart in her throat, but she managed. "How did I ever imagine I could walk away from you?" she wondered. "From this?"

"Walk away?" He looked startled. "You were going to walk away?"

"I didn't know how, especially after I fell in love with you."

"Okay, stop. I have to see for this." He scrambled around on the nightstand for his glasses and jammed them on. "Say it again."

"I thought it'd scare you off," she whispered.

"Seeing?"

"No." She laughed. "The words."

"Hey, nothing scares me." He rolled his eyes when she sent him a long look. "Okay, so it was a valid fear." He put his forehead to hers. "I'm so sorry. You are going to marry me, aren't you? Make me the luckiest man on earth?"

She pulled back. "Have you given thought to what you'd be marrying into? My father. My mother. *Serena*. The tortuous Monday-night family dinners—"

"I can deal with any of it, all of it." He tugged her into his arms. "As long as you're part of the package. Say you will."

"I will. Oh, Wes, I so will."

They sealed the vow with a long kiss, then Kenna pulled back and smiled. "Can I have my clothes, now?"

He ran his gaze over her and slowly shook his head. Then he tossed her back down, following her with his long, hard, powerful body. "Not...quite...yet."

_____ **Epilogue** _____

KENNA SAT in her new office in the Teen Zone. It was the same size as her Mallory Enterprises office had been, which meant barely big enough to breathe in, much less work in, but she loved it.

She was surrounded by stacks of paperwork, but she loved that, too. She knew what each stack needed, and what to do, and she was working her way through them.

With a grin on her face.

That was what happened when one finally got the right job, she supposed, you walked around with a stupid, goofy smile and drove people crazy because you were so ridiculously happy.

Lyssa poked her head in the door.

"Hey, there," Kenna said.

"So you did it." Lyssa's eyes were shuttered with the anger-sadness-perpetual irritation of a teenager.

"Did what?"

"Finished the classes you needed to be a counselor here for real."

Kenna tossed her pencil aside and leaned back. "Yep."

"I suppose that's why this came." Lyssa straightened and brought her hands around to the front, hands that were filled with a bouquet of wildflowers. "From Wes. The card says he loves you. Yech."

Kenna laughed. "Oh, love grosses you out, now?"

"It's just that you're *soooo* over the moon for him. I mean, it's embarrassing. You've only been dating him for like—I don't know."

"Two years," Kenna said.

Lyssa sniffed. "That's not long enough to be so over the moon."

Kenna laughed. "Two years is pretty long."

"Is he really your Prince Charming?"

"Well, I hope so, since I'm marrying him this weekend." Hard to believe but she, the unconventional, slightly erratic, definitely different Mallory was going to marry a suit—the cool, calm, boardroom man, Mr. Weston Roth.

She was really going to say "I do," move into his little house on the beach...

And have wild, reckless sex whenever she wanted.

She couldn't wait.

Serena had married Josh the year before and claimed marriage was better than anything she could imagine, even better than say...sex in a hot tub. And from Serena, that was quite an endorsement.

Not that Kenna trusted her cousin any more than she used to, but she was looking forward to proving that marriage was awesome all on her own.

"It's not too late to back out, you know."

Kenna laughed in shock. "Lyssa!"

"Kidding. I do like him, he's cute." The teen lifted a shoulder. "For an old guy, anyway."

"He's thirty-five."

"Like I said, old." Lyssa put the flowers on the one free corner of Kenna's desk, then looked around the room with disdain. "My bedroom might actually be bigger than this. You should complain."

"I like it." She and Sarah had painted the room in a soft rose, trimmed it in white. There were pictures on the wall, one of her and Sarah covered in said rose paint, one of Sarah with a bunch of the kids, and one of Kenna, Wes and Josh.

That one was her favorite.

"So..." Lyssa nodded toward the complicated-looking forms in front of Kenna. "Whatcha doing?"

"Trying to get us a grant."

"Why? Your dad is rich as God."

"Lyssa." She had to laugh. True to his word, her father had donated her Ferrari money, and with it, over the past two years, they'd spruced the place up and even added two full-time staff—herself included. "This one will get us enough money to get another Teen Zone across town."

"Who cares about them?"

"I do," Kenna said gently. "And Sarah does, and everyone who works here. We want as many kids as possible to get to come to a place like this—" She looked up and saw Wes standing in the doorway.

Her heart tipped on its side. Pathetic that it still did that, but she figured it boded well for the marriage.

And especially the honeymoon.

He gave her a slow smile that spread warmth through her body. "Ready?"

"For what?"

His smile widened to a naughty grin behind Lyssa's back, and Kenna blushed.

Blushed.

"Um...yeah." She stood. "We have to go...."

"Where?" Lyssa wanted to know, looking back and forth between them suspiciously. "Ah, man, you have that stupid grin on your face, too," she said to Wes. "Jeez, I'm so outta here."

When they were alone, Wes took Kenna's hand and pulled her close for a hug.

"What are you doing here?" she asked.

"I needed to clear my head."

"Uh-oh. Work driving you mad? Who is it, my father or Serena?"

"The thought of you, Mrs. Roth."

"Hey, I'm not Mrs. Roth, yet."

He pulled back and looked into her eyes. "Regrets?"

"Are you kidding? The only regret I have is not deciding sooner that you were worth my time."

"Ah. Speaking of that, when *did* you decide?"

"I think it goes all the way back to when I pulled you into the pool."

"Really, and why is that, almost-Mrs. Roth?"

"Because," she said with a grin as she set her head on his shoulder, loving that he made her feel feminine just by holding her. "That's when I saw you all wet and annoyed for the first time. You look good all wet and annoyed, Wes. You look real good."

He laughed and hugged her tighter, and she felt at home in his arms as she'd never felt anywhere else. "I love what you've done here," he said. "What you've done for the kids. And I also love—"

"What, this chartreuse-colored sundress?" With a smile, she pulled free and preened and danced in a little circle for him, knowing darn well one needed sunglasses just to look at her.

"Nope." He smiled into her frown. "What I love is you, Kenna. Always you."

* * * * *

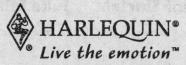

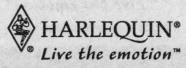

Forrester Square

LEGACIES . LIES . LOVE .

*Award-winning author Day Leclaire
brings a highly emotional and
exciting reunion romance story to
Forrester Square in December...*

KEEPING FAITH

by

Day Leclaire

Faith Marshall's dream of a "white-picket" life with
Ethan Dunn disappeared—along with her husband—
when she discovered that he was really a dangerous
mercenary. With Ethan missing in action, Faith found
herself alone, pregnant and struggling to survive.
Now, years later, Ethan turns up alive. Will a family
reunion be possible after so much deception?

*Forrester Square...
Legacies. Lies. Love.*

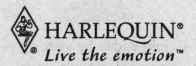

HARLEQUIN®

Live the emotion™

Visit us at www.forrestersquare.com   PHFS5

If you enjoyed what you just read,
then we've got an offer you can't resist!

Take 2 bestselling love stories FREE!
Plus get a FREE surprise gift!

Clip this page and mail it to Harlequin Reader Service®

IN U.S.A.	IN CANADA
3010 Walden Ave.	P.O. Box 609
P.O. Box 1867	Fort Erie, Ontario
Buffalo, N.Y. 14240-1867	L2A 5X3

YES! Please send me 2 free Harlequin Flipside™ novels and my free surprise gift. After receiving them, if I don't wish to receive anymore, I can return the shipping statement marked cancel. If I don't cancel, I will receive 2 brand-new novels every month, before they're available in stores! In the U.S.A., bill me at the bargain price of $4.24 plus 50¢ shipping & handling per book and applicable sales tax, if any*. In Canada, bill me at the bargain price of $4.94 plus 50¢ shipping & handling per book and applicable taxes**. That's the complete price—what a great deal! I understand that accepting the 2 free books and gift places me under no obligation ever to buy any books. I can always return a shipment and cancel at any time. Even if I never buy another book from Harlequin, the 2 free books and gift are mine to keep forever.

151 HDN DU7R
351 HDN DU7S

Name _____ (PLEASE PRINT)

Address _____ Apt.#

City _____ State/Prov. _____ Zip/Postal Code

* Terms and prices subject to change without notice. Sales tax applicable in N.Y.
** Canadian residents will be charged applicable provincial taxes and GST.
All orders subject to approval. Offer limited to one per household and not valid to current Harlequin Flipside™ subscribers.
® and ™ are registered trademarks of Harlequin Enterprises Limited.

FLIPS03

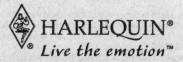

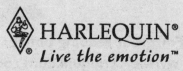